Weirdly Beloved

Tales of Strange Bedfellows,
Odd Couplings, and Love Gone Bad

Cynthia Ceilán

The Lyons Press
Guilford, Connecticut

An imprint of The Globe Pequot Press

For my eternal
KB

*Would we have loved each other so
had you been born a man?
or I a dog?*

To buy books in quantity for corporate use
or incentives, call **(800) 962–0973**
or e-mail **premiums@GlobePequot.com.**

The Lyons Press is an imprint of The Globe Pequot Press.

Text design by Sheryl P. Kober
Spot photography throughout © Photos.com and Shutterstock
Library of Congress Cataloging-in-Publication Data is available on file.

ISBN 978-1-59921-403-0

Printed in the United States of America

10 9 8 7 6 5 4 3 2 1

Table of Contents

Acknowledgments

I am a very lucky woman. After only ten or fifteen years of therapy, I'm beginning to think I'm going to be all right.

I'm lucky, too, to have amassed such a vast collection of good friends, some of whom I'm related to by blood. They are people who make me laugh, who let me cry, who listen to my stories, and who happily tell me theirs. I'd like to convey my thanks most especially to Matthew Rofofsky, Robert Cruz (you'll always be Bobby to me), Ernie Koy, "Annie Em," and, as ever, Gary and Terry Martin.

There are many others who shared with me their hapless tales of love and woe, some of which made it into in this book in one form or another. These are, for the most part, people who prefer to become famous some other way, so I can't list their names. To each of them I've sent a very special thank-you postcard.

You're welcome.

I will always be grateful to my editor, Holly Rubino, for being such an enthusiastic and cheery ally in this process. Many thanks also to Jim McCarthy, my brand new agent, the sweetest "bad guy" I've ever met.

And to Christopher, my very own weirdly beloved, who reminds me to thank him at least once a week. So thank you. Again. For real.

Introduction

> Although I cannot
> lay an egg, I am a very
> **GOOD JUDGE**
> of omelets.
> —GEORGE BERNARD SHAW

I was well into my adulthood before I realized that not everyone comes from an enormous family. I grew up surrounded by legions of aunts, uncles, cousins, little brothers, pets who were like siblings, godparents, real parents, great-aunts, great-uncles, grandparents . . . there were thousands of us. To us, a distant relative was somebody who lived in a country we hadn't yet visited.

Our "nuclear family" included people who weren't even remotely related to us, by blood or by marriage. If you lived next door to us long enough, you automatically got sucked into the fold. There were people I've always thought of as Auntie This or Uncle That, but as far as I can tell, our only common ancestors were Adam and Eve, or more likely, the Cro-Magnons.

We gathered frequently to celebrate everything, and sometimes made up excuses rather than wait for a legitimate occasion to throw a good party. I have an uncle who once baptized his dog. His next-door neighbor stood proudly as godfather.

For the most part, it was quite a wonderful way to grow up, being part of such a vast familial community. These warm, wonderful people had the power, by their mere presence, to make me feel safe and loved. They greatly influenced the adult I was to become, and probably had something to do with the fact that I now live with a semicomatose dog and rarely leave the house.

There were, inevitably, a handful of relatives with whom I would simply never see eye to eye. Among these was the mercifully small sect I've come to think of as "The Old Aunts." They're not all my aunts in the strict genealogical sense, and they're not all old, but that is how I think of them.

In the world of Old Aunts, there is only one way to fall in love, one way to be properly married, and one way to suffer the necessary indignities of wedded bliss. Old Aunts argue that "things were different" in their day, that "people knew how to behave" back then. They look at their beautiful young nieces with their fresh faces, pierced belly buttons, and trendy tattoos, and condemn their decadence in righteous shouts and whispers. "Disgraceful!" "Scandalous!" "A tragedy."

They forget, these Old Aunts, that their own mothers and grandmothers once dared to expose their ankles in public, bob their hair to their earlobes, and run away with foreigners. They will deny with their dying breath that anyone close to them was ever sent away to live with her own Old Aunt for a few months while the poor disgraced girl's menopausal mother pretended to have conceived a "miracle baby," who would grow up believing that his real mother was his sister.

Now there's a tragedy.

I'm not sure I would have been happy to learn that my own daughter had mutilated herself with indelible ink and multiple body piercings, but I'd like to believe that I would have been capable of loving her without the pitiless condemnation of an Old Aunt. Fortunately, this is not a dilemma I will ever have to face. All of *my* children are imaginary.

In real life, I am the wildly adored auntie of seven wonderful, flesh-and-blood, uniquely quirky nieces and nephews, and as of this spring will become a great-aunt for the first time, God help me. Technically, I suppose that makes me an *aunt* who is *getting older*. But I'll be damned if I'm going to be an Old Aunt.

For a long time now, I have been secretly hoping to someday become worthy of the title Weird Aunt Cindy, in the tradition of my beloved Aunt Betty, my flamboyant Aunt Saró, and my brilliant Aunt Carmen—fabulously strong and loving women who have never been afraid to express an unpopular opinion and who never met a pair of high heels or showy piece of jewelry they didn't like. My fear is that I could become both—Old *and* Weird. I know all too well that the two are not mutually exclusive, and that this is much too volatile a combination.

Weird Aunts are easier to love. Nobody quite understands their outrageous sense of style, the strange books they read, or their refusal to "be normal" (whatever that means), but we love them anyway. At the very least, we tolerate their eccentricities and promise to look after them when they lose the rest of their marbles.

But Old Aunts . . . those can be scary. The good intentions of an Old Aunt are too often held together with barbed wire and decades of rage. Their love and alleged concern for your well-being can shred you to tatters.

It was, in fact, after a typically thorny conversation I recently had with an Old Aunt I hadn't seen since I was a child that I was inspired to embark upon the fact-finding expedition that would ultimately become this book. This particular Old Aunt's notions regarding the state of modern love and relationships would have ordinarily left me in a daze of befuddlement and exasperation, which would inevitably lead me to stew for a few days in the bitter juices of my own confusion and hurt feelings. I decided instead to put all that bad energy to good use.

I set out to show that there is never only one way to fall in love, to endure or nurture a love, to celebrate and cherish a love, and most importantly, that there is no method too weird or outlandish to finally end a love gone bad. Who are they, these Old Aunts—who are any of us, really—to attempt to shame anyone who chooses to love in a manner that might be a little bit different? Or to deny that love, in all of its glorious irrationality, hasn't touched us all at one time or another, or changed us for the better? Even a bad love has the power to make us more courageous and compassionate human beings—if we find the strength to end it, survive it, and dare to love again.

The stories that follow are the result of the quest that began in the twisted branches of my magnificently gnarled family tree and then expanded to include a broader community— my neighborhood, my city, my country, my planet—and a span of time beyond the past and present of my own colorful family history. And because I have a tendency toward being easily crushed under the weight of my own guilt and concern for fairness, I even rummaged through my own desperately cluttered inner closet and dusted off a few decrepit skeletons. What I found in all these places will likely wilt the starchiest of my Old Aunts, maybe even finish a few of them off.

The tragedy.

Cynthia Ceilán
New York City
February 14, 2008

CHAPTER ONE

Strange Bedfellows

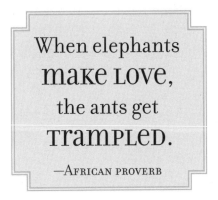

When elephants **make love,** the ants get **trampled.**

—AFRICAN PROVERB

In the realm of romance, the most frequently asked question is, "Do you love me [or him or her]?" The second is, "*Those* two got *married*?!"[1]

These are questions I have often pondered—or blurted out loud—at various times throughout my life. Mostly I've wondered these things about my own parents.

The fact of the matter is that the world has always been full of people who fall in love with each other for reasons none of the rest of us can quite fathom. Those reasons, I believe, are the finely woven strands and fibers so delicately enmeshed in the fabric of a relationship that they are simply invisible to the uninformed eye.

In some ways, a strong and healthy relationship can prosper by the "opposites attract" theory. In just about every rela-

---

[1] Results based on unscientific poll. Source: me and two of my girlfriends.

tionship, there is a partner who is a little—or a lot—more dominant than the other. Children have been known to benefit from having one strong Sherman tank of a parent (usually, but not always, the dad) to roughhouse and toughen them up in preparation for dealing with an often brutal world. The softer, more nurturing parent (usually, but not always, the mom) teaches them that the world can also be a kind and gentle place. She also keeps the dad from accidentally dropping the kid from a tree.

Nature always seeks a balance. Balance helps to ensure the survival of a child, not to mention the species. If both parents are brutes, or if both are fussy, overprotective nervous wrecks, then the only ones to profit from that relationship are the therapists and/or bail bondsmen in that poor kid's future.

Still, some unions are truly mystifying in that quest to seek the perfect equilibrium.

Take, for example, the case of Chang and Eng, the original "Siamese Twins." They really were from Siam (now Thailand) and were born joined at the chest by a thin strip of flesh. It is rumored that an American reporter once asked the two if they were particularly close, to which Chang responded, "I thinking we about five inches close."

In the early to mid-1800s, the brothers won fame, earned their fortune, and traveled the world with a series of carnival sideshows. In an unusual turn of events for so-called freak show entertainers of their day, Chang and Eng ultimately took control of their own destiny, successfully managed themselves, and prospered without the aid of the P. T. Barnums of the world.

Chang and Eng eventually gave up the circus life and settled in rural Wilkesboro, North Carolina. In an attempt to further cement their lives as normal, everyday members of their community, they became American citizens, bought a farm and a few slaves, and adopted the perfectly ordinary name of Bunker.

I'm sure they blended right in.

The Bunker boys were of wildly different dispositions and temperaments. They were hardly ever seen speaking to each other, leading many people to believe that they communicated telepathically. The truth is that they didn't really like each other very much. On those occasions when they did speak, it was often to argue over their preferences in everything from food to fundamental life philosophies.

Chang was the more ill-tempered of the two and had a bit of a drinking problem. Eng was quieter and more cerebral, and preferred a healthier lifestyle. During one particularly heated argument, Chang went

> *Chang was the more ill-tempered of the two, and had a bit of a drinking problem. Eng was quieter and more cerebral, and preferred a healthier lifestyle.*

so far as to threaten Eng with a knife. Thankfully, Chang realized just in time what a tragic mistake that would have been for them both—the world's first semiaccidental murder-suicide.

But here's the thing that fills me with wonder: From the moment of their conception until the day they died, these two men never experienced a single moment of true privacy. Yet they managed to work out an arrangement—not just between themselves, but with two other women—that allowed each brother to have his own love life.

In 1843, Eng married the lovely Adelaide Yates, a large and fearless brick wall of a woman. On the same day, Chang wed Adelaide's sister Sarah, a somewhat more retiring and less imposing human being. There are, sadly, very few photographs of the happy foursome, but there is one famous family snapshot taken about ten years into their respective marriages, a picture that speaks volumes. The sisters sit like bookends on either side of their conjoined husbands. The rather hefty Adelaide sits on the left, looking a lot like she could rip a tree stump out of her front yard with her bare hands. Sarah, a bit more demure and rather thin by comparison, sits on the right, scowling tensely through her eyebrows and the nearly invisible line of her lips. The brothers, of course, stand with their arms around each other, Eng on the left striking a brave and noble pose, and a smirking Chang on the right looking like he just drank dinner.

The photograph was not exactly the best endorsement for blissful love, but wait. There's more.

The Yates girls were the daughters of a local minister, which in itself is quite remarkable. That these good Christian girls married conjoined Asian twins in a time and a place in which interracial marriages were considered aberrant, immoral, and, in some cases, illegal, is absolutely extraordinary. I don't know for a fact whether marriages between "freak-show people" and "regular folk" were also illegal in North Carolina in those days, but I understand there was quite a bit of frowning-upon and rock-throwing when news of their impending nuptials got out. The Yates girls and the Bunker boys didn't let any of that stop them. They got married anyway.

Something about that makes me want to cheer.

But let's not overlook the fact that, in these couples' most intimate moments, there would never be fewer than three people.

Think about that for a moment.

Vivid, isn't it?

Each of the brothers had his own house, separate but within reasonable walking distance of one another. Each sister always lived in her own husband's house. Every three days, the brothers alternated their living and sleeping arrangements so that each one would get to spend time in his own home and have a turn at living with his own wife and family.

Yes. They each had a family.

Between them, Adelaide and Sarah bore a total of twenty-two children. It is generally assumed that Chang fathered ten of them and Eng the other twelve. The actual paternity of each child, however, remains somewhat shrouded in mystery. The names of all the children were listed in the family Bible in no particular order and under the names of all four parents.

I love this story on so many levels.

As the old saying goes, there's a lid for every pot. No four people ever embodied that sentiment better than Chang and Adelaide and Eng and Sarah.

I'm not quite sure what to make of another pair of strange bedfellows I came across in my search for weirdly beloveds, but I'll tell you their story anyway.

In 2006, there was a woman named Wook Kundor from northern Malaysia who, at the age of 104, married a man named Muhamad Noor Che Musa. He was thirty-three years old at the time.

Wook had been through quite a few husbands in the century or so that she had roamed the earth. Twenty, to be exact. Muhamad was the twenty-first man she promised to love until death did them part.

When asked why he had chosen such an elderly bride, Muhamad responded that he felt sorry for Wook, who, despite her many marriages and remarkable age, was childless, old, and alone. He clearly wasn't after her money, because, well, she didn't have any. If there was a physical attraction or sexual connection between them, Muhamad was too much of a gentleman to mention it. All he wanted for his new wife, he said, was to teach her how to read and write, and for her to teach him about religion.

Sometimes, I guess, love really is as simple as that.

Sarah Knapton and Kyle Kirkland, both twenty-two-year-old college students, have stood before a Montana judge hundreds of times and said, "I do," but never to each other. Not exactly.

Sarah is a professional bride and Kyle a groom for hire. They get paid $50 apiece for standing in as proxies for couples wishing to get married but who can't make it to the church (or the courthouse) on time.

This cottage industry emerged in 2003 when an American soldier serving in Iraq wanted to marry his pregnant Italian girlfriend. The soldier's parents hired a lawyer named Dean Knapton to find out whether it was true that Montana allowed double-proxy weddings, or if that was just a rumor.

As it turned out, it was true. The law had been on the books for decades, since World War II, most likely established in an age when many soldiers learned they had impregnated their girlfriends during that magical night of desperate passion before heading off to battle. In those days, when people "had to" get married, a proxy wedding was precisely the sort of narrow escape that kept respectable families from having to disown their impure daughters and illegitimate grandchildren.

Since the news of Mr. Knapton's little discovery got out, people from every corner of the world have been contacting the county clerk in Kalispell, Montana, to ask about scheduling double-proxy weddings, including people who have never donned a soldier's uniform or set foot on American soil.

The Montana State Legislature got busy revising the law in 2007. They didn't abolish the law altogether but restricted it to serve only Montana residents or active members of the U.S. armed forces.

One of the most incomparable unions by far has to be that of Christelle Demichel and her fiancé, Eric, who were married in Nice, France, in February 2004. Christelle showed up for her civil ceremony dressed entirely in black. Eric was unable to attend the ceremony because he was dead. Christelle's fiancé was a police officer who had been killed in a traffic accident in 2002. But that didn't stop the wedding.

According to French law, a live person can marry a dead one so long as the still-living half of the couple can prove that there was serious intent to marry before one of them passed away. Christelle was able to produce all of the required legal paperwork, which the couple had completed just prior to Eric's untimely demise. And so, under the law, Christelle

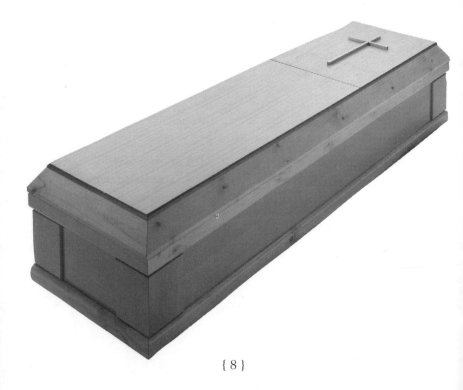

was wed—and widowed—all in a single breath the moment she said, "I do."

Brian Tandy, from Berkshire, England, was a man in love with the earth's mineral deposits. A geologist by trade, he devoted much of his time to the study of stone. When he passed away, it seemed only fitting that his wife turn him into a rock.

Brian died in 2003. Some months later, his widow, Lin Tandy, sent some of the ashes to a company in the United States called LifeGem, which promised to turn the cremains into a "diamond." These yellow-hued crystals are then cut and polished to resemble precious gemstones and can then be mounted on a ring or other piece of jewelry that can be handed down as heirlooms to the generations to come. Lin Tandy was purportedly the first person in England to use such services.

Some of LifeGem's customers express fears or concern over the fate of their cremains once their own children or grandchildren pass away. Who wants to hang on to great-great-grandmother's urn, or that poor spinster uncle's cremains? They figure chances are better that their ashes won't end up on a pawn broker's shelf or in some landfill in New Jersey if the ashes can be turned into something of perceived monetary value for the offspring of generations yet to come.

Lin Tandy is deeply comforted by the fact that she can "wear" her husband and take him with her wherever she goes, and that one of her daughters will someday inherit this remembrance of her father. She has already arranged to have her own ashes turned into a LifeGem so that the other daughter can wear her mother on her finger for the rest of her own life.

Sometimes it's really hard to just let go.

Swans are well known not only for their grace and beauty, but for their natural instinct to remain faithful to their mates throughout their lifetimes.

I recently came across the tale of one such creature, a beautiful black swan that took up residence on Lake Aasee in Münster, western Germany, in the spring of 2006. The local residents named her Petra.

Petra fell madly in love with a giant, white, plastic paddleboat. The boat was built to resemble a white swan. It was easily five times bigger than she was. It would be like me falling in love with that statue of Abraham Lincoln in Washington, D.C., if he looked less like Abe Lincoln and more like somebody I actually found sexy.

Petra followed that paddleboat around everywhere it went all summer long. Nothing could separate her from the object of her love. Whenever anyone tried, Petra became hysterical.

The residents of Lake Aasee and vicinity, not to mention the owner of the paddleboat, were utterly enchanted by Petra's devotion to her chosen mate. But they began to worry about what would happen to her at the end of the season when the boat would have to be removed from the lake for the winter. Peter Overschmidt, the owner of the boat, didn't have the heart to separate the two, and soon the town came up with a plan.

The residents took up a collection to finance the couple's relocation. The boat was paddled along a canal that connected Lake Aasee with a pond at the Münster Zoo. Petra, of course, paddled right alongside her mate through the whole journey. The two settled easily into their new home, where they could safely spend the winter.

The zookeepers hoped that Petra would lose interest in the paddleboat at some point, or when she met some of the more eligible (and responsive) SBMS's (single black male swans) that already resided at the zoo, but she would have none of that. She spent the entire winter by her true love's side. In the spring, she returned with him to Lake Aasee, to the utter delight of the town's residents and tourists.

Petra and the paddleboat are still together, despite rumors that she had a short-lived affair with a live duck. Perhaps she was only trying to make the paddleboat jealous or was frustrated by her love's indifference. Nevertheless, they spent the second winter back at the Münster Zoo in 2007.

All of that will change soon, though. The town is now arranging to build a permanent cold-weather shelter for the couple on the very shores of Lake Aasee, where Cupid's arrow first struck Petra right between her star-crossed eyes.

We'll never know for certain whether the great love that blossomed between two of the world's tiniest known people happened as spontaneously as it did for Petra and her paddleboat, or whether it was the result of another one of those great P. T. Barnum machinations. Maybe it was purely a matter of logistics, a question of supply and demand. Or perhaps it was some combination of all the above. Whatever the case, things seemed to work out quite nicely in the end.

Charles Sherwood Stratton was born on January 4, 1838. He was a big baby, too, weighing more than nine pounds at birth. When he reached fifteen pounds and twenty-four inches in length, his growth all but stopped. He grew only in the tiniest increments throughout the rest of his childhood and adolescence. In his adulthood, he never measured more than forty inches tall.

The world would later come to know Charles Stratton as General Tom Thumb, the tiny little man made famous by P. T. Barnum and his traveling circus.

Except for his size, Charles's development was otherwise normal. It was as if nature had decided to make a perfect reproduction in miniature of an ordinary man.

In 1863, he met Lavinia Warren, another one of P. T. Barnum's "finds" and whom Barnum had named Little Queen of Beauty. At the age of twenty-one, Lavinia was thirty-two inches high and weighed twenty-nine pounds, even tinier than the man she would soon marry. She, too, was a perfect woman cast in miniature form.

Their wedding was a much-ballyhooed affair and made international headlines. Even President Abraham Lincoln and his wife, Mary Todd, sent them a wedding gift and later honored them with an invitation to the White House for a special dinner. The ceremony took place at Grace Episcopal Church and was followed by a lavish reception at the posh Metropolitan Hotel in New York City. The maid of honor was Lavinia's even tinier little sister, "Minnie Bump." The best man was one of Charles's costars in Barnum's traveling show, a thirty-inch-tall man known as "Commodore Nutt."

The "Thumbs" greeted their guests standing atop a grand piano. More than two thousand people showed up to catch a glimpse of the magical little couple. Charles and Lavinia were together for twenty years, until his death in 1883.

Lavinia's teeny-tiny wedding shoes, adorned with embroidered roses, can be seen at the Smithsonian Institution in Washington, D.C.

In a very unfortunate (and sadly creepy) twist of fate, a young man and woman from London met, felt an instant affinity for each other, fell in love, and got married. Shortly after their wedding, they found out they were siblings.

More horrifying still was the fact that they were fraternal twins, separated at birth and raised by different adoptive parents.

The case came to light in December 2007, as lawmakers, child placement experts, and fertility specialists heatedly debated the pros and cons of allowing open records in cases of adoption and requiring more detailed documentation for births resulting from egg and sperm donations.

A court annulled the couple's marriage as soon as it was discovered that they were brother and sister. Their identities, of course, were kept secret for obvious reasons.

No one knows for certain what became of these two unfortunate creatures. My heart breaks for them both.

Some people search the world over for the love of their lives, only to find him or her ambling about in their own backyards.

Something like that happened to a Chinese shepherd named Bao Xishun. Bao's work among the livestock in his Mongolian village made it somewhat difficult for him to meet new women. Now in his late fifties and unwilling to resign himself to the lonely life of a bachelor, Bao placed personal ads in outlets all over the world. He was determined to find a wife.

A pretty young woman named Xia Shujian responded to Bao's ad, and they decided to meet.

Xia turned out to be about half Bao's age, and when she stood as straight as she could, the top of her head just barely reached the crook of his elbow. It came as no surprise to Xia to learn that Bao was listed in the *Guinness Book of Records* as the world's tallest living man. At seven feet, nine inches tall, Bao is almost two and a half feet taller than Xia.

It seemed that destiny had decided to intervene in this union. One of the things that drew them to each other was the discovery that they had been born in the same village, a place called Chifeng.

Bao was already famous, even before he married Xia, and for reasons not exclusively related to his place in the *Guinness Book of Records*. In December 2006, Bao was asked by desperate veterinarians to assist in a somewhat unshepherdlike task.

Some dolphins at an aquarium in Liaoning Province had become sick after biting off and ingesting pieces of plastic around their pool. Doctors were unable to remove the obstructions with their normal instruments, but Bao had no trouble sticking one of his very long arms into the mouths of the dolphins to retrieve the offending matter, a maneuver that surely saved the dolphins' lives.

When the media got hold of the story and learned of Bao's engagement to Xia, everyone wanted to get into the act. At least fifteen different companies offered to sponsor a lavish wedding for the couple.

Early in 2007, the bride and groom decked themselves out in traditional ceremonial robes trimmed in gold. Bao rode in a two-camel cart to the place where his bride-to-be waited for him—in front of the tomb of the thirteenth-century Mongolian emperor Kublai Khan—and then proceeded with her to the wedding site.

Thousands of people attended the elaborate ancestor-worshipping ceremony of lucky Bao Xishun and Xia Shujian.

The forces of fate and nature can also play some interesting tricks in the name of love. Lynette and Fred Debendorf, a couple from Mears, Michigan, had been married nearly thirty years. While walking along the shore between the Silver and Pentwater Lakes one day in the early fall of 2007, they came across a bottle in the sand. Inside was a rolled-up piece of paper.

The message in the bottle was written by newlyweds Melody Kloska and Matt Behr of Wisconsin. They had written their marriage vows on the piece of paper, along with their names and address. They tossed the bottle into Lake Michigan and watched it float away.

When the Debendorfs found the bottle, they were astonished to find that they and the Wisconsin couple shared the same anniversary: August 18th.

The Debendorfs wrote to the newlyweds to wish them well and let them know the fate of their message in a bottle. Melody and Matt, who had each been married several times before and had been wary for years of tying the knot again, took this as a good sign that they had finally made the right choice.

Here's what I learned from studying these stories and, most especially, from observing my own parents' marriage: Love, far from being blind, is the process by which our eyes are opened to the one wondrous gift that no one else has ever noticed about the person with whom we choose to spend our lives. Beyond physical attraction, equitably negotiated living arrangements, or similarities in mind, body, and spirit, it is that one lovely gift that impels our love and devotion toward another human being. Strange bedfellows see in each other what the rest of us miss.

I say that makes them a damned sight luckier than normal bedfellows.

CHAPTER TWO

No, **YOU'RE** *Just a Dog*

> I care not for a
> man's religion whose
> dog and cat are not
> the BETTer for it.
>
> —ABRAHAM LINCOLN

A mere two years into the first seriously grown-up relationship of my young life, my sweetie decided he'd had just about enough of me whining, "But we never *do* anything together anymore!" So he got me a Pomeranian.

We named her Kitty Bo, after one of his cousins.

He was much too polite to say so at the time, but I know he got me that dog just so that I'd stay out of his hair while he finished figuring out how to become Master of the Universe. Unfortunately for him, instead of one less female yapping in his ear, he ended up with two. But he was right about all the rest. Kitty Bo turned out to be just about everything I could ever have wanted in a husband.

Before I go any further, let me just say that I am perfectly aware of how utterly carried away some pet owners can get.

I know for a fact that it was not so long ago in the history of our civilization that a dog's primary function was to be night watchman of the homestead, herder of sheep, and retriever of dead duck. Cats were little more than cheap exterminators.

Somewhere along the way, these former members of the animal kingdom became our children—not *like* our children, our actual *children*. They are our soul mates and confidants, heirs to our fortunes. We dress them in bright yellow slickers when it rains and slip-proof booties when it snows. We build them little butt rickshaws when they get hip dysplasia and buy specially made strollers when they're too old or too fat to walk very far but still like to get out for a little fresh air and people-watching in the park. We happily buy them plane tickets and schlep them all over the world in fashionable, airline-approved carry-on bags so we can show them Paris in the spring and visit Grandma and Grandpa at Christmas, where there had better be a toy under the tree for the grandpuppy—or else.

> *I know, I know. You're probably thinking, "These poeple are nuts! They're absolutely ridiculous!" And until I became one of them, I used to think so, too.*

To say something like, "It's just a *dog,* for crying out loud!" to someone who shares a life with such a wildly adored creature is to risk death and dismemberment—at the hands of the owner, not the dog. These cherished companions are not *animals,* they will tell you unequivocally. They are little hairy people with slight speech impediments.

I know, I know. You're probably thinking, "These people are nuts! They're absolutely ridiculous!" And until I became one of them, I used to think so, too.

It was Kitty Bo who taught me that there is no such thing as "just a dog." A great-niece of Prince Charming II, the only Pomeranian ever to win Best in Show in Westminster's 132-year dog-show history, she was every bit the princess her neurotically inbred bloodline dictated she should be. Even so, she was smart as a whip. Funny, engaging, expressive, unrelenting in her demands for attention, affectionate beyond words, and utterly theatrical in her frequent and extreme displays of joy, boredom, sadness, impatience, devastation, belligerence, and adulation. There was never an unexpressed emotion between us. Best of all, she was absolutely fascinated by my every move. She would fly into fits of ecstasy over the simplest things, like me showing up, or whenever anybody made a noise that sounded like a spoon stirring a pot. Through the guilelessness of simply being her sweet psychotic self, she changed my life forever.

I remember one night in particular when I came to bed somewhat later than usual, having spent half the night writing some strange story or another. I tiptoed into our bedroom and was about to turn off the night-light when I was struck by the tableau before me. There was my aspiring Master of the Universe, hogging the whole bed, flat on his back, mouth agape, spread-eagle, snoring away with wild abandon. And in her bed in a corner of the room was Kitty Bo, also flat on her back, front legs curled over her chest, hind legs splayed wide open in a decidedly unladylike manner, snoring in perfect syncopation to her daddy's night noises like a tiny Greek chorus.

I watched them for a long time, overcome with an immense sense of gratitude for having them in my life. "Nobody who doesn't feel safe and loved can sleep this recklessly," I thought. It made me feel good to think that maybe I'd had something to do with creating such a home for my odd little family. In that perfect moment of my life, I felt profoundly secure in the knowledge that there was nothing else I needed or wanted from the world. It was all right there.

And so it was for at least three more years.

In the end, it was Kitty Bo and I who would grow old together.

For nearly a century in dog years, we were inseparable. We argued and fussed at each other like old ladies, cracked each other up, kept each other warm, and worried ourselves to tatters whenever the other was sick. I would have walked through fire for that little creature. I'm pretty sure she would have done the same for me—not that I would have let her. It was a pure and unquestioning love, exquisite in its simplicity, utterly devoid of doubt, regret, or reproach.

We don't know for sure what ever became of Kitty Bo's dad after I threw the sonofabitch out. She eventually stopped waiting for him, hour after heartbreaking hour, watching for any sign of movement through the glass panes that framed our front door until she fell asleep in the foyer or it was time for us both to go to bed. There was nothing I could do to dissuade or distract her. In time, I too got over the habit of listening for the horrid mechanical grind of the garage door, wondering whether there was enough clean underwear in his drawer, or worrying whether he had eaten dinner yet. All of that came to matter less and less as the days and weeks crept by and got behind us. What mattered to us always was that she and I had each other.

And as crazy as I was about that maddeningly exigent, prissy little poufy-haired thing, as wonderful and loving a companion as she was to me for all those years, it's still a bit of a struggle for me to understand what would compel a person to marry his parrot.

There's an actual place, MarryYourPet.com, where you can go to pledge your undying and eternal devotion to the hairball, lizard, or guppy of your dreams.

Dominique Lesbirel of Renkum, Holland, hosts this strangely wonderful Web site. There is a "Priest Matilda" who performs the ceremonies online, offering a choice of three wedding packages to the oddly betrothed.

The simplest ceremony is the equivalent, I guess, of a Las Vegas quickie. For ten bucks, you can pledge allegiance to your pet and get a nice certificate made from "100% real paper."

If you prefer a larger wedding, $35 will get you the certificate plus an I MARRIED MY PET T-shirt, so that when you wear it, the whole world will know what you've done.

Then there's the super-duper deluxe package, which will set you back about $200. In addition to impressing the virtual pants off your pet, you get the certificate, the T-shirt, and a hand-embroidered, personalized wall plaque in which your name, the name of your creature, and the date of the nuptials are lovingly cross-stitched.

The "vows" are a rather reasonable and appropriate listing of rules and responsibilities. I was, frankly, quite relieved to read this one: "This union is a marriage of minds and companionship. You have no conjugal rights. If you want to consummate your marriage, we suggest you share some cake."

I'd like to believe that most of the people who visit this Web site and actually go through with the wedding do so in the spirit with which it's intended: to acknowledge and revel in the fact that our four-legged, winged, and scaly companions often inspire us to such extremes of devotion that, to the rest of the world, we appear quite demented—but that's perfectly okay with us.

The testimonial pages at MarryYourPet.com are full of happy love stories, many of which were clearly written with tongue firmly in cheek. I have no doubt that all of the stories were inspired by the real-life relationships people have had with their well-loved pets. This just isn't the sort of thing a non-pet owner could ever make up.

I fear some of the stories, however, are dead serious.

"I've pretty much given up on women," said Bill in telling of his beloved Timmy, a sick and frightened little dog he found on the street as a puppy and nursed back to health. After seven years together, Bill decided to marry him. "With Timmy it's different," he explained. "We don't talk or do much, just walk in silence . . . For me, there's no better partner."

Maybe it's a good thing Bill never found a wife. Timmy certainly owes his life to that simple fact, and Bill may have unwittingly spared some hapless woman the horror of living with a man whose idea of a perfect relationship is one in which he's not required to "do much" and involves a lot of "walking in silence." Still, stories like these reaffirm my belief that life often finds a merciful way of sorting everything out for the best.

It would appear, however, that life was on vacation that week in February 2006, when Charles Tombe from the village of

Juba in Sudan was caught in flagrante delicto with his beloved Rose, who, unfortunately for her, was a goat.

Mr. Alifi, Rose's rightful owner, awoke in the middle of the night to a frightful noise. When he stepped outside his hut to investigate, he found Mr. Tombe and Rose locked in a passionate embrace. Mr. Alifi shouted, "What are you doing there?!" causing Mr. Tombe to lose his balance and fall off Rose. Acting quickly, Mr. Alifi was able to capture and subdue Mr. Tombe until someone in authority could arrive.

Mr. Tombe later stood trial before a council of village elders, who determined that he should pay Mr. Alifi a dowry of 15,000 Sudanese dinars (about $50) for having besmirched Rose's honor. And, in the tradition of southern Sudan, Mr. Tombe was then ordered to marry the female he had deflowered. That she was a goat was apparently beside the point.

Charles and Rose Tombe were together for just over a year. My guess is that Charles was a little more happily married than Rose.

Tragically, poor Rose died quite suddenly in May 2007. She choked to death on a plastic bag while scavenging for food. It could not be determined whether the death was the result of Charles's poor skills as a provider, Rose's less-than-healthy eating habits, or if she had just had enough her husband's weirdness and finally decided to end it all herself.

Poor Rose.

And if I were Mr. Tombe's neighbor, I'd be keeping a very close eye on my chickens.

Sometimes nature shakes things up a bit by turning the tables on weird animal-human unions.

In 2007, an unnamed sixty-year-old Australian woman was given a camel as a birthday present. The gift was, apparently, something she had always wanted. The camel seemed happy with the arrangement, too. He was so, happy, in fact, that when he started feeling a little amorous, he decided to make his new owner the object of his affection.

Horrified friends found the woman crushed under the weight of her 330-pound pet. The animal, also not named by the news source, was found resting in the standard camel postcoital position on top of the flattened woman.

Believe it or not, some people marry animals for much weirder reasons than love, or even lust.

There was a little seven-year-old girl named Shivam Munda from India whose father arranged for her to marry a dog. You see, Shivam's upper teeth appeared before her lower ones. The Santhal community to which she belonged considered this a very bad omen, portending certain and impending doom.

Marrying a stray dog would release the child and her family from the curse.

Fortunately, Shivam will be free to marry a regular human being when she gets older. We might have to wait a few years to see if the anticurse remedy worked, and if Shivam will, in fact, let her father arrange her next marriage.

However, we know right now how things turned out for Phul-ram Chaudhary, a seventy-five-year-old Nepalese man whose Tharu culture holds similar beliefs. He, too, married his dog, in accordance with local custom, to ensure good luck and a long life. Mr. Chaudhary, whose upper and lower teeth had come in—and fallen out—many years before, suddenly grew some new teeth at this late stage of his life. The custom holds that, in such instances, the old man must take a dog as a bride to ward off misfortune. So he married his dog in a wonderful, cheery ceremony surrounded by friends and family.

Three days later, he was dead.

I'm no doctor, but maybe those weren't teeth growing back in the old man's head. He probably should have gotten that checked out.

For the slightly (very slightly) more conventional pet lover, a pet-dating agency is now open in Krasnoyarsk, Siberia.

Yelena Tulaeva is a wedding planner and pet-matching consultant. She helps her customers find the perfect same-species mate for their domestic animals, then arranges a formal ceremony and reception in compliance with "all wedding traditions," including proper bride and groom attire. All of the animal brides, of course, are dressed in white.

I wonder how she attaches the veil to the head of a python. Or how she can tell the difference between a boy and a girl turtle.

Of course, most animals find a mate just fine without our assistance. And God doesn't seem to mind that they don't save their virginity or get married in white. In fact, the so-called lesser species appear to handle courtship, reproduction, and parenthood in a much more civilized manner than we do.

Few creatures are more committed to their partners than our fine feathered friends. It's estimated that about 90 percent of the approximately 9,700 known bird species choose a mate for life and raise their babies together. Many couples have also been observed returning to the exact same nesting site every year.

Choosing a mate for life doesn't necessarily mean that they're all monogamous, though. Boy birdies like visiting other girl birdies' nests—and the girl birdies like it. However, the males do return to the mother of their chicks after each dalliance and are diligent about helping with the nest-keeping and the child rearing. In all likelihood, a couple of the hatchlings in the nest probably belong to one of the mama bird's boyfriends anyway. Open marriages are, apparently, a widely accepted practice in bird land.

One notable exception, however, can be seen among black vultures. They not only mate for life, they have a zero-tolerance policy in place when it comes to infidelity. If one horny vulture decides to peek under the skirt of another vulture's wife, every vulture in the immediate vicinity will beat the crap out of the philanderer.

During the few years I lived in Atlanta trying very hard (and mostly unsuccessfully) to impersonate a suburbanite, I was fortunate to have witnessed a very beautiful sort of avian union.

I had a bird feeder on the back deck of the house, which overlooked a lovely wooded area. Lots of birds of many different varieties came to visit and eat their fill of the seeds and treats I loaded into the feeder just so I could watch them from my window.

Two birds in particular caught my eye, a husband-and-wife pair of cardinals.

I knew that female cardinals are less ostentatious in appearance than their more brightly colored mates. My little female cardinal was a more subdued shade of auburn compared to her husband's beautiful fiery-red plumage.

I noticed that the female never flew up to the feeder. It was always the male who picked up a beakful of seeds and brought them to whichever spot on the deck floor she chose to wait for her dinner. He'd fly back and forth, pouring the seeds onto a little space between them, right at her feet, like an offering. She ate delicately but with a hearty appetite. He made as many trips back to the feeder as necessary until she had eaten her fill. Only then would he fly back and eat his own dinner directly from the feeder. Afterward, they would both fly away together, back into the woods, until the next day when they'd return and do it all again. I could set my watch by their ritual.

At first I thought she was some kind of pampered wife, and he was just beak-over-tail-feathers in love with her despite her unwillingness to get her own birdseed. Other cardinals who visited my backyard, male and female, always ate directly from the feeder. But then one day I noticed what was different about this couple: The female had a bit of a handicap. She was missing the toes at the end of one of her feet and was unable to grasp the perch at the opening of the feeder or balance herself properly on her little matchstick stump of a leg.

I burst into tears like an idiot as soon as I saw that.

What a lucky little girl bird, I thought, to have found such a kind and generous mate. I wondered if anyone would ever spit food at my feet so I wouldn't starve to death if I lost my toes. I couldn't imagine anyone ever loving me that much.[2]

I moved away eventually, although I fear the damage to my psyche was permanent. I never forgot those cardinals, though. And ever since, I've found myself from time to time seeking out similar stories of love and devotion in the animal kingdom.

Silly and strange as some of these stories may sound, the more I hear of them, the more convinced I become that animals sometimes have more sense—and bigger hearts—than people. They certainly have more sense and heart than we're willing to give them credit for.

I remember seeing a story on the news sometime back in the mid-1990s about a husband-and-wife pair of house cats that had been expecting a litter of kittens. The kittens all died either shortly after birth or were stillborn. The mama cat was inconsolable. So the papa cat went out into the woods behind the house, found a couple of newborn bunnies, and brought them to his wife.

---

[2] Suburban life made me a little squirrelly sometimes.

The mama cat nursed the bunnies and cared for them as if they were her own. The bunnies looked like they were crapping their pants in abject terror, but I saw how utterly gentle that mama cat was handling them.

You must admit there is a certain intelligence at work here, something beyond instinct. The papa cat figured out that the mama cat was truly suffering the loss of her babies, so he went out and found her some new ones. He could just as easily have eaten them on the way back home and lied about where he had been all afternoon.

If he had done nothing at all, we would have thought nothing of it, because we wouldn't have expected a cat to solve such a complex emotional and logistical problem. But the fact that he did, and in a manner that seems so beyond coincidence, is what makes this such an interesting occurrence.

I still wonder whether the papa cat went out specifically searching for kittens and, finding none, brought back the baby bunnies as substitutes. The little rabbits were approximately the same size as newborn kittens, although their white fur and pink eyes stood out in stark contrast to the mama cat's brown and gray stripes.

I wonder, too, what the mama rabbit did when she found that two of her dozen or so newborns were missing. Did she notice? Did the papa cat fight her for the two bunnies, or did he just swipe them at the first opportune moment?

I wish I knew. I also hope the cats' predatory instincts didn't kick in until the bunnies were fast enough to get away.

There was a similar story in the news more recently, in the summer of 2007, from a city called Mamurras in Albania. Three newborn puppies were orphaned when their mother was struck and killed by a car. A cat from the same household had just lost her own newborn kittens. She adopted the puppies and, in doing so, saved their lives by giving them her milk. In the process, she probably ameliorated some of her own feelings of loss over the death of her kittens.

And just this morning I saw another such story on the news. A dachshund named Tinkerbelle from the heart of America's farmland has adopted a baby pig and suckles it right along with her own newborn puppy. The piglet, named Pink (derived from Pig and Tink), was the smallest and weakest of twelve siblings born prematurely. Tink had recently given birth to two puppies, but one of them was stillborn. Her owners got the idea to let her foster the poor little pig when they saw how well she did with a couple of her newborn "nephews"—puppies from a much larger litter recently born to another dachshund in the same household.

I don't know what that farmer is feeding his animals, but there appears to have been a whole lot of baby making going on all over that farm in the last few months.

Oddly enough, Tinkerbelle seems to have chosen the piglet as her favorite, cuddling and nuzzling it while the other puppies jockey for prime milking positions. Meanwhile, Pink the Piglet looked smugly adorable in the midst of his new family and is in fine health.

New mothers in the animal world are not the only ones willing to overlook the occasional physical differences of little creatures from other species who happen to find themselves in need of some attention. At a wildlife center called Pennywell Farm in Devon, England, there's a ruggedly handsome dog, a boxer named Billy, whose tough-guy exterior belies a heart of pure mush. Billy has become friend, protector, and constant companion to a little goat named Lilly. Lilly was abandoned by her mother just hours after she was born.

Caretakers at Pennywell Farm fed Lilly from a bottle. Billy the Boxer's protective instincts kicked in the moment he laid eyes on her.

Lilly adores Billy the way a little sister idolizes a big brother. She follows him around everywhere he goes. Billy loves her, too. He entertains her, watches out for her, and licks her face clean after she eats.

If this is nothing but pure animal instinct at work, I wish we humans had a little more of it.

CHAPTER THREE

Crazy for You

> When you live in the shadow of insanity, the appearance of another mind that thinks and talks as yours does is something close to a blessed event.
>
> —ROBERT M. PIRZIG

Rush-hour traffic in Atlanta defies all laws of physics, logic, and nature. It is, thankfully, one of the relatively few places on the planet Earth where bumper-to-bumper traffic can actually move at a hundred miles per hour—unless, of course, someone pulls over to change a tire, in which case the Rubberneck Effect kicks in and turns your fifteen-mile commute into a four-hour belly crawl through the corridors of hell. From outer space, the outbound lanes of the city's highways in the evenings must look like an enormous nest of psychotic, metallic snakes fighting to break free from their tangled point of origin, Spaghetti Junction. To survive that twice-daily trek to and from work, you have to have fourteen eyeballs, the cold-blooded resolve of a Roman gladiator, and a sphincter like a steel trap.

I'm not quite built that way.

The soothing voices of Noah Adams and Mara Liasson, cohosts of NPR's radio program *All Things Considered* in those days, went a long way toward helping me stay calm and focused during those nightmarish drives home. I especially looked forward to the stories of the show's rotating roster of essayists and commentators. One of my favorites was Elissa Ely, a psychiatrist who worked at a state mental institution in New England.

One day her story was about two long-term residents at the facility, a man and a woman too psychologically and emotionally fragile to survive on their own in the unforgiving world that existed beyond the hospital walls. They found each other in this sad place, and from their union emerged one of the most beautiful love stories I have ever heard.

The woman, Dr. Ely explained, was plagued by the relentless voices of her many personalities, and moved from one moment to the next amid the bluster and flurry of her own incessant chatter. The man who loved her had not uttered a single word in many years. In each, they had found their perfect other.

I listened to the kind voice and poignantly astute observations of Dr. Ely as she summed up this unlikely relationship: "In his silence he adored her, and she loved him with all of her selves."

For some reason, those words opened up a floodgate of emotion within me. I blinked away tears and clutched at my heart, gripping the steering wheel with my other hand and sobbing like an idiot. I would have pulled over to the side of the road to weep if the maneuver had not required me to change lanes. I cried all the way home. And as I pulled into the driveway, I made the solemn vow that my next husband would be a lunatic.

In my saner moments, I've often scared myself to pieces by some of the men I've found sexy.

The most erotically charged scene in cinematic history, as far as I'm concerned, is the one in which Hannibal Lecter, from his cage in that municipal building in Memphis, passes Clarice Starling's files back to her. She reaches for them, and for the briefest of moments, he holds fast to the manila folders. And then, ever so tenderly, he brushes the back of her hand with just the tip of his index finger.

I wish I could spell the noise I made the first time I saw that.

Even thinking of it now, after having read *Silence of the Lambs* and watched the movie so many times that I can recite the dialogue verbatim, the memory of that moment still sends wicked little chills down my spine.

I am horrified by this on so many levels.

First of all, the bug-eyed, unblinking, pasty-faced Hannibal Lecter is not exactly what anyone could call Hollywood handsome, despite the fact that, in real life, Anthony

Hopkins is quite the distinguished-looking gentleman and, as a young man, was a total cutie. Secondly, mere minutes after that fingertip caress, Hannibal Lecter ate the face off that poor policeman, and then he eviscerated his partner, that other poor policeman. And how can we forget that this was a deranged CANNIBAL! A butcher of humans! A brilliant and unnervingly serene, murdering sociopath! And unbelievably ugly!

Oh, but that tender brush of his fingertip against the back of Clarice's hand just about made me lose consciousness the first time I saw it, and still makes me smile every time I think of it.

Sick. It's just sick. I'm just a sick, sick kitty.[3]

And here I am, all these years later, still smiling, utterly a-tingle.

There must be a similar moment in the lives of previously wholesome, decent, normal women who fall madly and inexplicably in love with real-life homicidal maniacs. Surely there's something—a gesture, a look, a word—something so powerful and instantaneous, so jarring that their lives and their outlooks are forever changed. How else to explain this phenomenon?

---

[3] Not something I've discussed much in therapy, probably because, deep down, I kind of like this about myself.

I can almost understand—almost—the attraction to a Ted Bundy or a Scott Peterson. If a person knew nothing about the horrific crimes of these men, the sheer evil of their actions and motivations, that person might be inclined to say, "Now *there's* an attractive fellow. I wonder if he can dance the Pachanga?"

But these women knew everything the rest of us knew about those cold-blooded killers. Bundy had an entire fan club of women vying to marry him, right up until the moment Florida prison officials strapped him into Old Sparky and threw the switch. Peterson wasn't on death row for a whole hour before he received his first proposal of marriage. By the end of his first day in prison, there were no fewer than thirty-five wannabe-the-next-Mrs.-Petersons beating a creepy path to his jailhouse door. Lyle and Erik Menendez, those adorable parent-slaughtering brothers, have both been married in prison—Lyle twice! And all three brides were, by all appearances, lovely normal-looking young women.

But fat, clown-suit-wearing John Wayne Gacy? And evil, hairy, disgusting, stupid, ugly, child-killing Richard Allen Davis? And Satan-worshipping Richard "the Night Stalker" Ramirez, for crying out loud? All of these repulsive, horrifyingly depraved fiends have had women throwing themselves at them from the moment their names and images were first emblazoned on the front pages of our newspapers and splashed across our television screens.

Sheila Isenberg, who interviewed thirty women for her 1991 book, *Women Who Love Men Who Kill,* says that, typically, such women crave excitement and adventure. What bigger thrill is there, she posits, than not knowing whether the love of your life will be allowed to make that phone call tonight, or whether he might be executed tomorrow, or whether he'll end up languishing in prison for thirty or forty years, or escape next week just to be with you, his one true love?

The inmate, of course, is starving for attention of any kind, but especially welcomes the female variety. And, unlike those citizens who have earned the right to roam the earth as free and productive men, the inmate has all the idle time a person could ever want. This makes him much more likely—not to mention willing and able—to lavish all of his attention on a woman in love with him, and in ways that few men in her past might ever have done.

And the payoff for her? She has the love and devotion of a famous man, and—best of all—he can't get out and hurt her. Of course, he usually can't get out and touch her, either, but who ever said love doesn't come with its share of sacrifices?

Not all women who fall in love with the world's Menendez brothers and Scott Petersons are emotionally fractured, victimized females, as Ms. Isenberg suggests. Some are intelligent, well-educated, self-sufficient women who are convinced that their dearly beloveds are innocent of the crimes for which they've been convicted. Others believe more passionately in redemption and second chances than they do in the death penalty.

Such was the case of a California woman who worked for a drug treatment center in the 1970s and made the acquaintance of a convicted murderer in San Quentin. This man had decided to devote what was left of his misspent life to a prison program designed to keep youngsters out of trouble. She was so impressed by his intelligence, charm, and devotion to his cause that she befriended him. The more time they spent together, the more she realized she was falling in love with him. She married him in 1977.

Lucky for them, his death sentence was later commuted to life in prison. And by an even luckier stroke, he was released from prison altogether in 1985. She divorced him immediately afterward.

Perhaps it was that he wasn't as attentive or chivalrous with her when not under the surveillance of heavily armed guards. Maybe he hogged too much of the bed, or grossed her out by hanging his dirty underwear on doorknobs. Or, just maybe, as is often the sad case in marriage these days, after only eight short years of courtship and a couple of months under the same roof, the thrill was simply gone.

> She once told a reporter from the San Francisco Chronicle, "It's too hard for me to try to figure out why other women would do this."

This woman has spoken often of her marriage to the former inmate, but only under the condition of anonymity so as not to jeopardize her career. And probably also because her ex-husband is still out there somewhere, unshackled.

She once told a reporter from the *San Francisco Chronicle,* "It's too hard for me to try to figure out why other women would do this." She said she knew many others who had married condemned inmates, and, in her opinion, those women had "lost their marbles." Her love, on the other hand, was as sane as it was real. She became enamored with this inmate for the "unusual, interesting," and "charismatic man" that he was.

Apparently, he ceased being interesting and charismatic the moment he moved into her house.

One woman who isn't as reticent about revealing her name or losing her job is Isabelle Coutant-Peyre. When madame was a mademoiselle growing up amid wealth and privilege in France, she received her education in some of that country's most prestigious Catholic schools. She grew up to become a well-respected lawyer—until she was hired by Carlos Ilich Ramirez Sanchez, better known as Carlos the Jackal.

Carlos earned his reputation as one of the world's most feared and hated assassins in the early 1970s. A dark and glamorous figure who frequented embassy cocktail parties, he was, among other things, the mastermind behind the horrifically brutal murders of eleven Israeli athletes at the 1972 Olympics in Munich, Germany.

It took nearly thirty years, but he was finally captured in 1997 and imprisoned for the murder of two French policemen and an informant. It was during his stay at Le Sante prison in Paris that he made the acquaintance of the lovely Isabelle, now a successful and accomplished woman in her forties. She described her fifty-two-year-old client as "an exceptionally warm man."

Madame Coutant-Peyre married the Jackal in a Muslim ceremony, in a bleak and filthy prison room in 2001. Carlos recited some verses from the Koran, he and his new wife signed a piece of paper, and he gave her a platinum Cartier ring.

The kiss they exchanged during the ceremony is the closest they have come to actually consummating the marriage, which isn't exactly legal because, as it turns out, Isabelle never quite got around to divorcing her husband, and Carlos was still legally married to his second wife, a Palestinian woman named Lana Jarrar, who disappeared many years before and was never seen or heard from again. But it's all okay with Isabelle and the Jackal because, as she is quick to explain, the marriage is recognized by Muslims all over the world. That's good enough for her.

During a television interview in 2003, Mr. Jackal calmly acknowledged that he was responsible for the deaths of more than fifteen hundred people in the name of Palestinian liberation. This is the same man who writes excruciatingly mournful poetry to his beloved wife, filled with sentiments such as, "I am jealous of the sun that tans you / Of the shade that caresses you / Of your sheets that do not cover me."

Isabelle feels confident that she and her Jackal will someday have a real wedding ceremony and a union that is recognized by the law. "When he's free," she says.

She must be one hell of a lawyer.

Interestingly, the inverse of this jailhouse phenomenon is practically nonexistent.

There are approximately fifty women on death row in this country right now. None of them are getting hot and horny letters from male groupies anxious to marry them. To have virtual sex via correspondence, yes. Lots and lots of letters for that. Proposals of marriage, no.

It should come as no surprise, then, that women behind bars have begun to marry each other.

In March 2007, six Florida corrections officers allowed two female inmates to exchange vows in the prison's Close Management Unit. The ceremony, officiated by another inmate, was, by all accounts, quite lovely. The wedding accoutrements included pink bows made from prison forms and a wedding cake constructed from various dessert items from the pantry. The brides exchanged rings woven from someone's dreadlocks and a little dental floss. The bride who wore the veil was "given away" by another female inmate.

Six officers at the Lowell Correctional Facility were suspended, one guard was fired, and another guard resigned. Sergeant Jennifer Thomas, the one who resigned, accused prison officials of being prejudiced against same-sex unions, which are still largely frowned upon in Florida. Marriages between heterosexual murderers and normal people are okay, but not conjugal visits.

Meanwhile, in more liberal California, San Quentin conducts wedding services for its inmates on the first Friday of every even-numbered month. At every one of these ceremonies, an average of twenty male convicts marry women who are madly in love with them. There is always at least one death row inmate among the grooms at every ceremony.

I'd like to believe that I don't begrudge anyone the right to fall in love. Still, I can't help feeling some measure of comfort knowing that these relationships are all taking place behind barbed wire and electrified fences.

There's a rather rare but endlessly fascinating mental condition known as folie à deux, which roughly translates into something like "loony times two." It's what happens when one person's delusions infiltrate another person's reality, in effect making the other person crazy, too.

Imagine a man who thinks he is Napoleon Bonaparte. He is so convincing that his wife then comes to believe that she, of course, must be Josephine. In literature, Don Quixote and Sancho Panza had the perfect delusional partnership. Don Quixote thought he was a knight, and his faithful servant, Sancho, followed suit by acting as his valet.

As far as the two people in the "*folie*" are concerned, all is right with the world. They're in perfect harmony with each other and the world they've created for themselves. It's everyone else who fails to see the beauty of their chosen reality.

Sometimes this phenomenon occurs in groups of greater numbers, as in *folie à trois* (a trio of mad folk), *folie à famille* (a whole houseful of them), or *folie à plusieurs* (too many to count). Some professionals cite notorious mass murderer Charles Manson and his "family," as well as Adolph Hitler and his merry band of Nazis, as classic examples of *folie à plusieurs*.

Interestingly, once the chief loony is removed from the picture, the mental state of the second and subsequent deluded souls often returns to something that actually resembles normal, or whatever passed for normal in their pre-*folie* state.

The most curious case of *folie à deux* I've ever come across was documented in a 1992 article by Robert Howard in the *American Journal of Psychiatry*. The *deux* in this instance were an elderly woman and her exceedingly loyal dog.

The woman, an eighty-three-year-old widow, believed that her noisy upstairs neighbor had somehow figured out how to transmit what she called "violet rays" though her ceiling. She was convinced this man was trying to hurt her and her beloved doggie. The proof, she said, was in her sprained back and the chest pains she began to experience the moment the evil neighbor put his sick plan into action. Also, the dog had begun scratching himself much more vigorously, she said, especially at night, when, as everyone knows, violet rays are at their deadliest.

To protect herself and the dog, she built herself a shelter by putting her mattress under the kitchen table. She hid there whenever she heard the neighbor moving his death machine around upstairs. She also built an equally impenetrable fortress for her dog out of some old suitcases. She then began teaching the dog to run for cover whenever they heard the man upstairs. The dog, of course, obeyed and soon began showing actual signs of fear and distress whenever the neighbor moved around in his own apartment.

What the old woman managed to do was alter the dog's perception of the world to match her own deluded version of it. She redefined for the dog what was dangerous and what was not, in effect sharing her madness. The dog certainly couldn't know about "violet rays" and evil neighbors, but he knew about picking up on people's emotions and states of mind. He also knew that, in this particular pack, the old lady was the "big dog" and, therefore, must be trusted to know things that he didn't. The pooch accepted the version of reality presented to him by his boss and then acted accordingly, just like Sancho Panza.

Linda and Burton Pugach are a New York City couple who are the very embodiment of crazy love. In fact, Dan Kloris made a documentary film about them in 2007 and called it exactly that: *Crazy Love.*

Burt was clearly off his rocker long before he first set eyes on the beautiful twenty-year-old Linda Riss sitting on a park bench in the Bronx in the late 1950s. He pursued her gallantly and relentlessly, despite the fact that he was already married and had a child. He wooed her with gifts and nights out on the town, wild rides in his flashy convertible, and promises that the wife and child were but a minor—and temporary—inconvenience. He swore he was working to divest himself of them as quickly as possible.

After a couple of years of Burt's over-the-top seductions and empty promises, Linda finally ended the relationship.

> *Burt went to jail for about fifteen years for that little display of affection. In the meantime, Linda tried unsuccessfully to find love elsewhere.*

One evening in 1959, Burt knocked on the door of Linda's Bronx apartment claiming that he had, at long last, an engagement present for her. When she opened the door, he threw lye in her face, partially blinding her and permanently disfiguring her. As the years progressed, Linda lost her eyesight altogether.

Burt went to jail for about fifteen years for that little display of affection. In the meantime, Linda tried unsuccessfully to find love elsewhere.

When Burt was released from prison, he once again showed up on Linda's doorstep, begging her to marry him.

And she said yes.

Even more astonishing than this is that they're still together. Linda spews vitriol at him almost constantly in repayment for what he did to her and everything he took away. Yet she is completely dependent on him, and he is convinced that she adores him.

In their own twisted way, they seem to be made for each other.

The adage "Love is a form of insanity" is often attributed to the Marquis de Sade, the psycho who tried to convince us that pain equals fun. Anyone who has ever been madly and passionately in love knows that he was right, at least about the insanity part.

What's truly amazing is not just that we're all susceptible to this phenomenon of inexplicable transformation from sane to deranged, but that we can more or less continue to function in the "normal" world even when we're in the throes of such madness.

Some other horribly jaded soul once remarked, "The cure for love is marriage."

I think I'd rather be crazy.

CHAPTER FOUR

I Love My Stuff

> I love Mickey Mouse
> **more THAN**
> **any woman**
> I've ever known.
>
> —WALT DISNEY

The right pen gently cradled in the warm folds of my hand is a uniquely intimate experience for me. Make it a beautiful fountain pen and I'll practically lose consciousness with ecstasy.

A pen is the perfect instrument for certain kinds of writing—poetry, love letters, eulogies. Because we think faster than we can write, the pen forces the words to linger in our hearts and minds a little longer, where, in the process, they can gather great power. I doubt Shakespeare's sonnets would have been as evocative had he hammered them out on a PC.

Modern technology offers us the facility to dispense with all that flowery airy-fairyness by allowing our fingers to commit words to paper or screen at rapid-fire speed. It's efficient, recordable, immediately transmissible, and frees us

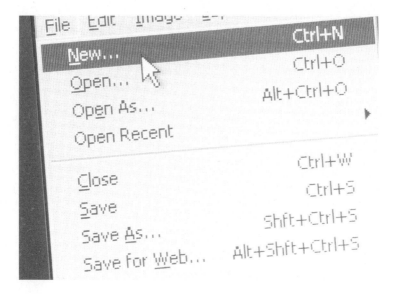

from having to memorize a bunch of dumb rules regarding spelling and grammar. This makes the computer keyboard or the handheld electronic device the perfect tool for business communications, hate mail, and cybersex.

Many of us who learned to type in the Decades of Darkness (before 1980) know something the rest of you may have sadly missed: There is something positively bewitching about writing to the *tappa-tappa-tap* of a genuine old-fashioned typewriter.

I was twelve years old when my father brought home an ancient Smith Corona from his office for me to play with, one of many that had been relegated to the trash heap to make way for a shipment of newfangled IBM Selectrics. I taught myself how to type on that horrid thing, which weighed more than my little brother and whose keys I practically had to hit with a hammer to make a readable impression on the page.

As I found myself hunting and pecking less frequently for the right keys, I began to make my peace with this intractable hunk of metal and its various moving parts. As my fingers developed their own muscle memory and I picked up a little more speed, I began to hear something rhythmic and oddly familiar in the sound of the keys striking the platen. I also liked the millions of tactile impressions on the backs of smooth sheets of paper, which tickled my fingertips when I tried to read them like Braille. Writing on a typewriter engaged almost all of my senses, but it was the *tappa-tappa-tap* that I found irresistibly hypnotic.

There is something about that noise in particular—entirely different from the muted and fake-sounding plastic *clickety-click* of a computer keyboard—that seems to open much more interesting doors in the twisted corridors of my imagination. While I appreciate being able to print unlimited copies on demand and make corrections with ease on my PC, the process leaves me vaguely dissatisfied in too many other respects. When I want to write something from the depths of my soul, I will invariably find myself yearning for the sound of the typewriter, whose echoes call to me like the memory of an old lover. I relish the knowledge that I can return to her as easily as if I had never left.

But for all the love I have ever felt for my various writing instruments, as much as I have marveled over those mechanical wonders and all the power I discovered at the ends of my own fingertips, I have never wanted to have sex with my Smith Corona.

I can't even imagine how I would begin to arrange myself for such an event.

There is a brand new disorder—or perhaps only a new name for a peculiarity that may be as old as mankind itself—called objectophilia. It is the mental health diagnosis conferred upon a person who has fallen in love with an inanimate object, like a toaster or a lamppost.

An objectophile derives feelings of love, sexual attraction, and gratification from things rather than people and can't imagine having that kind of relationship with a live human being.

Objectophilia is different from the "love" one would have for, say, a red Ferrari or an Orgaz-O-Matic waterproof cordless vibrator. It's a bit more difficult to make the case for the vibrator, but here's the main distinction: No matter how often you have sex with it, in it, or on it, neither the car nor the dildo can ever love you back, nor would you expect it to. If you can understand and accept that, then you're probably not an objectophile. You might be something else we'll discuss in another chapter, but not that.[4]

In some cases, it's not that difficult to understand how a person could develop strong feelings for an object, like the anonymous young man who sought relationship advice from his peers on the online support forum Conscious Loving when he began to fear there might be something wrong with him. Out of the blue one fine day, he realized he had developed deep feelings of love and physical attraction for his acoustic

---

[4] The deeper you go into the weirdness, the blurrier the lines get. For purposes of comparison, however, you might want to check out the transformation fetishists in Chapter 5. They're weird but seem able to function in the world with less medication.

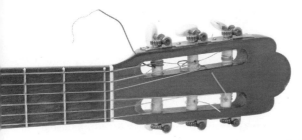

guitar. He was fully cognizant of the fact that this was not normal, but he couldn't help himself.

Most of the people who responded were kind and sympathetic, but very few of them seemed to get the point. The bewildered young man tried over and over to explain. "When I see a girl that I might be interested in," he wrote, "the thought that she would take time away from me and my guitar makes me shiver." He wasn't hiding behind the guitar to avoid a real relationship, as some respondents suggested; he actually *liked* the relationship he already had with his guitar and didn't want another. Most significantly, he believed the guitar's feelings were somehow reciprocal. "My guitar treats me better and makes me feel better than any woman ever has," he said.

And there's your smoking gun right there.

I can understand perceiving a guitar as "coming to life" when stroked or strummed in just the right ways and in all the right places. Its shape even mimics the classic curves of a woman. Still, there are enough clues here to indicate there's something just a *little bit* off the mark with regard to this particular young man's desire for love and affection.

There is a beautiful woman named Eija-Riita Eklöf-Mauer who lives in Sweden. On June 17, 1979, she married her dearly beloved. She lost him tragically when he was brutally murdered by a raging mob in November 1989. She watched the whole thing unfold on television.

> *Eija's wedding ceremony consisted mostly of going to the local government office and having her name legally changed to include Berliner-Mauer as a surname.*

Despite her many years of widowhood, Eija continues to use her married name, Mauer, which means "wall" in German. Her husband of ten years was—you guessed it—the Berlin Wall.

Sounds like a bad joke, I know, but it's true.

Eija's wedding ceremony consisted mostly of going to the local government office and having her name legally changed to include Berliner-Mauer as a surname. This is how she still signs her name.

Since earliest childhood, Eija has believed in animism, the belief that everything has a soul. As such, she is able to relate to objects in the same way that she relates to people. She sees all things as being alive. As Eija reached adolescence and physical maturity, the concept of animism flowed rather naturally into her awareness of herself as a sexual being.

Eija has managed to overcome her grief over the loss of the Berlin Wall by transcending the natural separation that often accompanies the death of a lover. She collects photographs and other memorabilia of the wall and has built several models of the structure. She frequently writes poems to her beloved, expressing such sentiments as, "I needed a strong support in my life . . . and I found YOU—my beloved Berlin Wall!"

Although she remains faithful to the true love of her life, Eija has often felt a strong sexual attraction to other objects. Of particular interest to her are structures that have some element of symmetry, such as railroad tracks, fences, gates, and bridges. "All these things have two things in common," she says. "They are rectangular, they have parallel lines, and all of them divide something. This is what physically attracts me."

The fancy German sexologist Volkmar Sigusch, former director of Frankfurt University's Institute for Sexual Science, has been studying people like Mrs. Berlin Wall for quite some time. Dr. Sigusch is not at all surprised by the emergence of this phenomenon. He has concluded that virtually every large city in the world is full of "singles, isolated people, cultural sodomites, many perverts, and sex addicts."

Clearly he has never visited an average American suburb.

Dr. Sigusch also asserts that animals fall under the category of "objects," and, therefore, people who want to marry their pets, for example, are also objectophiles.

Now, I'm no fancy German sexologist, but on this point I must disagree.

Animals, by definition, are not inanimate objects. With the possible exception of sea monkeys, most pets are capable of responding in kind to our displays of affection, as well as fighting back, running away, or dying of sadness when they are neglected or mistreated. In this respect, they're not so different from people. And they're definitely more engaging than a spatula.

On the other hand, people who have sex with animals are a lot of things I'm trying really hard not to say—like sick twisted bastards—but that still doesn't make them objectophiles. Those whose sexual proclivities include bestiality might only be objectophiles if the animal in question is now a stuffed owl or a moose head. If it's dead but not stuffed, then I'd think that makes the sick twisted bastard a bestio-necrophile (or something like that).

There was, in fact, a guy in Minnesota, Brian Hathaway, who ended up doing a stint in jail after he was caught having his way with a deer carcass on the side of the road in 2006. His lawyer tried to have the charge dismissed, arguing that his client was not guilty of bestiality, which is illegal in Minnesota, because the deer was dead, and therefore, "no longer an animal." It was, most assuredly, a very nice try. The judge disagreed that that's what the law intended regarding crimes against sexual morality. It also didn't help that, a year and a half before, Hathaway had pleaded no contest when he was charged with killing a horse so he could have sex with it.

It sets the mind reeling, doesn't it?

Another case study of Dr. Sigusch is a man named Joachim. At the age of twelve, he developed "an emotionally and physically very complex and deep relationship" with a Hammond organ. The relationship lasted for several years.

What turns Joachim on the most are the inner workings of technical or mechanical objects. This can pose a serious threat to his ability to remain faithful to his lover. A repair job on a radiator, for example, can easily lead to an affair.

Joachim currently maintains a monogamous relationship with his steam locomotive model train set.

Bill Rifka, a thirty-five-year-old psychology student, is in love with an iBook computer. To Bill, his laptop is clearly a male of its species. He acknowledges that that makes this particular relationship a homosexual affair, but this causes him absolutely no distress.

Of all of Dr. Sigusch's subjects, Bill seems the most well adjusted.

Some cases of sex with nonhumans straddle the fence, so to speak, between objectophilia and what might otherwise be categorized as simple, opportunistic semicrimes of passion.

Young Michael Plentyhorse from Sioux Falls, South Dakota, for example, was charged with a sex crime when he was caught trying to have intimate relations with a bald and mostly naked mannequin at the Washington Pavilion arts center in November 2005. It was, apparently, not the first time Michael had paid a visit to this particular lover. Guards at the arts center reported that they often found the mannequin in various stages of undress. It's widely believed Michael was the culprit behind each of those incidents.

A year after Michael's arrest, an appeals court ruled that Michael would not have to register as a sex offender after all. He was also found not guilty of indecent exposure since there was no one around to witness the actual exposure—except for the mannequin and the guard who found him with his pants puddled around his ankles.

Scottish cyclist Robert Stewart was not so lucky. The fifty-one-year-old was engaged in "sexually aggravated breach of the peace" with his beloved bicycle when the cleaning staff walked in on him at the hostel where he lived. Robert was wearing only a white T-shirt at the time. He was humping the bike so enthusiastically that he either didn't hear or chose to ignore the persistent knocks at his door. The housekeeper called the sheriff, and Michael was arrested. The court sentenced him to three years probation and required him to register as a sex offender for the duration of his probation.

Robert Stewart's case sparked much heated debate on a number of issues stemming from this odd arrest and conviction. Women in particular wondered if they could be charged with a sex crime if they happened to be caught by the sheriff or a nosy maid while enjoying a carefree moment of "stress relief" with a fully charged vibrator.

In another case in Scotland, this one in Edinburgh, thirty-eight-year-old Robert Watt was fined £100 in 1997 for trying to have sex with a shoe on a public street. In 2002, he was arrested again for sexually assaulting a traffic cone while a crowd of pedestrians watched. Some of them were horrified. A few found it rather entertaining.

Robert Watt's case attests mostly to the fact that some human beings will screw just about anything, whether or not it moves or has a pulse. Unlike Robert Stewart, who truly loved his bike, Robert Watt was just looking for any agreeable hole to poke, preferably in front of witnesses. It's not likely Watts was doing this for love, or for that matter, procreation.

Objectophilia extends far beyond the purview of mere mortals. In the fall of 1993, a fake deer caught the eye of a seven-hundred-pound bull moose. The results were tragic.

The Morrill family of Waterboro, Maine, had been using the foam-stuffed plastic deer as a target for practicing bow hunting. On that cold and lonely October day, the deer instead became the target of the moose's unbridled lust.

The Morrills videotaped the encounter between the two as the moose persisted in its attempts to impregnate the deer, even after its fake antlers fell off. The deer was eventually decapitated in the attempted copulation. The fact that the head and antlers were destroyed before the more obvious portions of the deer's anatomy make me wonder if the moose might have been attempting some sort of demented foreplay, or whether it didn't much matter to the moose which end of the deer got the business. It wasn't until the deer was little more than a pile of debris on the lawn that the moose finally gave up and wandered dejectedly back into the woods.

This was by no means an isolated incident. Moose have been known to become amorous with all manner of non-mooselike creatures, including cows, horses, lawn furniture, automobiles, and the occasional slow-moving hunter.

Meanwhile, elsewhere in this great nation, the Southwest National Primate Research Center reported that Gabriel, a male chimpanzee, became utterly obsessed with a leather boot. Gabriel wrested the article from a handler by grabbing her by the leg and fighting her until she relinquished her footwear.

Gabriel was frequently seen making wild, passionate monkey love to the boot, leading some to surmise that Gabriel was more likely to be a shoe fetishist than an objectophile. However, there are no reports that Gabriel has ever demonstrated any real interest in other people's footwear or other leather objects, or even the handler's other boot. He has never attempted to forcibly steal anyone else's shoes, either. He has apparently found his one and only.

If the concept of objectophilia in and of itself isn't extraordinarily strange enough for you, there may actually be a number of variations and subcategories that could reasonably fall under this collection of sexual and romantic predilections. One of them has been dubbed "mechaphilia." It is the form of objectophilia attached specifically to machines.

In 2003, an author who goes only by the name Schlessinger (no first name or initials) wrote a memoir about his experiences as a mechaphile. In it, he describes how he came to terms with this aspect of his sexuality and the relationships he has had with a variety of mechanical objects, such as the saucy little reel-to-reel tape recorder whose sexy curves stole his heart some years ago. Schlessinger's book, aptly titled *Mechaphilia: Sexual Attraction to Machines,* chronicles his adventures in all realms of his sexual universe, including encounters he's had with actual human beings. The most difficult aspect of his objectophilia, he says, has been gaining the acceptance and understanding of his family. He is otherwise perfectly at peace with his emotional and sexual attraction to machines.

Chris Donald, from the western United Kingdom, manages to take mechaphilia a step or two further. Chris's extreme attraction to motor boats, Jet Skis, and automobiles in particular once led him to have one of his car's exhaust pipes widened and rounded to better accommodate his anatomy. His "boudoir" is the heated and carpeted two-car garage attached to his home.

Chris has met many other mechaphiles online, some of whom are only voyeurs. They like to watch Chris "make love" to his car. Some of them videotape the encounters.

I don't know if there's a special word for those folks, the ones who like to watch, but they all seem rather normal once you've heard about Karl Watkins, an electrician from Worcestershire, England. Karl was jailed in 1993 for having sex with a paved stretch of road.[5]

If the thing you love most in the world is your own "thing," then boy, are you in luck.

Fun-filled and forward-thinking cities such as San Francisco, London, and Copenhagen have successfully hosted

---

[5] Ouch.

Masturbate-a-Thons. The event is exactly what the name suggests.

The first one took place in California in 1998. Much to my surprise, it took a little while for this event to catch on, but now the Masturbate-a-Thon is an annual occurrence. As of this writing, the latest one took place in Denmark in May 2008.

Organizers claim that one of their goals is to help break all those stodgy old taboos surrounding the ancient art of self-pleasure. Danish sexologist Pia Struck Madsen couldn't wait to welcome men and women from all walks of life to Copenhagen and usher them into the wonderful world of "pleasure, relaxation, and self-discovery."

Something tells me the participants won't need much ushering. They already know the way.

Typically, separate rooms are made available for men and for women, and also for those who prefer to share their sexual experiences without actually having to touch another human being.

If you think even for a moment that this event is the epitome of egomaniacal self-indulgence, you would be quite mistaken. The participants do it to raise money for their favorite charities. I don't know if the charities are aware of this.

In a rather interesting twist, some people have actually found a way of combining their fondness for self-love with a form of objectophilia. Maybe not on purpose or with a full awareness of it, but that is the net result nonetheless.

One of the best examples of this creative variation is the brainchild of Amber Hawk Swanson, a young woman in her late twenties who spent $12,000 to have a life-size clone of herself made in the form of a sex doll.

"Amber Doll" was put together by a company called Real-Doll, one of several companies that specialize in anatomically correct, lifelike mannequins specifically for use as sexual partners. The company offers several models, offering choices for different hair colors, skin tones, eye color, and other traits. The dolls all have realistically molded features, soft silicone skin, and adjustable joints. These playmates are nothing like your weird Uncle Herman's blow-up sex toys. Still, Amber wanted more.

She contracted with Cyber F/X, a Burbank outfit that caters to the Hollywood film industry. After completing a three-dimensional scan of Amber's face, they worked with RealDoll to create a mask that could be Velcroed onto the RealDoll head. The result was a sort of slightly smaller identical twin with a facial expression that can only be described as "pretty but dumb." Literally, there's nobody home.

It took about nine months to complete Amber Doll. The real Amber arranged to pick her up from the factory on her birthday, which further complicated the relationship. Real Amber now sees Amber Doll as some combination of lover, twin sister, and offspring.

Real Amber learned the hard way that *all* relationships require a certain amount of work. While Amber Doll is relatively low maintenance, at least compared to the average sex partner, there's not much she can do for herself. Her silicone skin is soft to the touch and can be warmed with an electric blanket, but it also attracts a lot of dirt, dust, and . . . well, let's face it, stray hairs. Amber Doll's ablutions involve a lot of lint-removal tape and cleaning solvents. Also, her face tends to fall off during rough play.

In January 2007, Real Amber took Amber Doll to Las Vegas to get married. They wore identical rented bridal gowns. "I only got one real look of disgust," she said of the reactions of passersby. Everybody else just stared.

I guess people in Las Vegas have seen weirder things.

It's entirely possible that there's only one person who could ever have made Amber and her custom-manufactured sister/daughter/wife look like your everyday, ordinary, garden-variety all-American couple. That person's name was Carl von Cosel.

Carl came to America in the 1920s, having left behind a wife and family in his native Germany. On his way to Florida, he stopped briefly in Cuba, inexplicably convinced that the love of his life was waiting for him there. He envisioned some lovely dark-haired Latin beauty merrily cavorting among the Carnival revelers and set about searching for her through the crowded streets of Havana.

Tired and despondent after four days, he gave up trying to find her and resumed his original quest, which was to begin his life again in a new land at the age of fifty-one. He boarded the ferry to Key West, where his sister awaited his arrival.

A few years later, while working at a hospital that was suspected of occasionally doubling as a brothel and speakeasy, Carl fell in love with a patient named Maria Elena de Hoyos, a beautiful twenty-two-year-old woman who was dying of tuberculosis. He had, at long last, found his lovely Latina.

Carl fancied himself a rather extraordinary inventor and concoctor of healing potions. With the permission of the young woman's family, he went about the business of saving her from what was, at the time, an incurable disease. Maria Elena died anyway.

> *In the dead of night (so to speak), he stole the body from the crypt. He kept her in his bedroom and slept with her every night.*

Carl convinced the de Hoyos family not to bury Maria Elena, but rather to let him inter her in a mausoleum. In their grief and somewhat grateful to Carl for his attentions toward their daughter, they agreed.

Unbeknownst to the family, Carl visited the corpse nightly, painstakingly treating it with formaldehyde and other preservatives. Eventually, he decided it would be easier and less risky to simply take the girl home with him. In the dead of night (so to speak), he stole the body from the crypt. He kept her in his bedroom and slept with her every night.

As Maria Elena's inevitable decrepitude began complicating the couple's relationship, Carl came up with ever more ingenious ways of holding her together. He wove piano wire into her now-exposed rib cage, filled her abdominal cavity with fragrant herbs, stuffed rags into her various saggy parts, and occasionally spritzed her with a little perfume. He also covered what was left of her skin with overlapping layers of wax and silk. As Maria Elena's hair fell off, Carl gathered it up and sewed it into a wig. When her eyeballs disintegrated, he installed a pair of glass ones into the sockets. And when her womanly parts were no longer usable, he fitted her pelvic cavity with a length of rubberized tubing.

It was Maria Elena's sister who, years later, discovered that her sibling's body was missing from the mausoleum. She immediately went to see Carl von Cosel and found what was left of Maria Elena's corpse lying in Carl's bed. She was clad in a rotting lace wedding dress and bridal veil.

Carl was arrested but could not be convicted of any crime. The statute of limitations on grave robbing had run out in the seven years he had kept his rigged-up bride in his home. Carl was allowed to go free. Maria Elena's family reburied her remains in an undisclosed location.

Carl lived another dozen or so years, but not exactly alone. In 1952, he was discovered dead on the floor of his own bedroom, clutching a life-size doll in his arms. The doll was wearing the wedding dress and death mask that once belonged to Maria Elena.

It just breaks your heart, doesn't it? The things we do for love . . .

Of all the sexual deviants, and with very few exceptions, objectophiles generally seem the most harmless. They're not interested in our children or our animals, or even our spouses. It's the lawn ornaments we might have to keep an eye on. Given a choice between an objectophile and a goat-humper, I'll take the thing-lover as a next-door neighbor any day. I'm certain I can get over the sudden disappearance of a plastic flamingo, although my dog's off-limits, of course, even in his semicomatose state. He only *looks* like a pelt. But I know he's in there.

What wonderfully interesting chats I could have on rainy afternoons with a sweet old objectophile neighbor. I can see it all so clearly: dear befuddled Mildred and I sharing a nice pot of tea, talking about her deep and abiding love for the hanging fern she keeps in her bedroom, or the torrid affair she once had with a weed whacker.

There's so much I'd want to ask her.

CHAPTER FIVE

Alternate Realities

> We know there are known knowns: There are things we know we know. We also know there are known unknowns: That is to say we know there are things we know we don't know. But there are also unknown unknowns—the ones we don't know we don't know.
>
> —FORMER DEFENSE SECRETARY
> DONALD "RUMMY" RUMSFELD

My first love was a doozy. Venus stretched one lithe, beautiful arm toward me, reached into my slack-jawed mouth, down past my throat, through my esophagus, and into my guts, then yanked hard and pulled me inside out while Cupid plinked a few crooked notes on a toy piano and laughed his diapered little ass off.

At the merest whisper of his name—the most sweetly strung syllables I had ever heard—my heart would stop and my eyes would roll back into my head. I was enraptured, mystified, in agony, in awe. I was out of my mind with love. I was twelve.

I don't know how I ever survived falling in love with David Cassidy.

It was me and fifty or sixty million other little star-struck girls in bell-bottom jeans, flowery and tie-dyed tops, and fringed vests, all of us beginning to show the first tentative signs of the years of acne yet to come. When we weren't busy planning our respective weddings to David, we spent inordinate amounts of time striving to achieve "Cher hair." This was the alternate universe we inhabited.

I knew I wasn't the only girl in love with the world's most beautiful boy, but I would not be persuaded to believe for a single moment that I wasn't the one David would ultimately pick as his bride. All the teasing and eye-rolling from people who should have known better—the grown-ups—served only to turn this into my *secret* love.

I saw David on TV a few months ago and realized two things: (a) I have become one of those awful grown-ups, and (b) I really was nuts.

He's still kind of cute, in a sad, vaguely nostalgic sort of way. But the more I looked at him, the happier I was that my emotional development progressed a bit past the age of twelve. I'm sure David would be equally relieved to know he didn't end up with me. It would otherwise have been just too weird for words.

Still, I remain in awe of the enormous power that first love exerts over all the rest of our days. I'm also somewhat saddened by the realization that no future love, no matter how real or sincere or good or right, is ever as magical as that very first one.

Each relationship takes a little piece of ourselves with it when it leaves. If we're lucky enough to find love in our later years, what our partners too often get is a somewhat dinged up and bandaged version of our original selves. A little older and wiser, yes, and with any luck, still willing to believe in the magic, but a bit too cautious about pretending not to know better. The wide-eyed, wide-open wonderment that pervaded our romantic babyhood is the little piece of ourselves that we lose to our first love. And with each subsequent romance, another chunk falls off.

> *Of course, I knew girls who, even at twelve, seemed to have gone straight from jump-rope games to French kissing with barely a heartbeat separating the two.*

As a formerly lovesick tweenie whose first love was an utterly unattainable boy-man who was cuter than any real boy I had ever known (and, weirdly, cuter than most of the girls I knew, too), I suppose it was only natural for me to wonder how often a person's very first experience of romantic attraction involves someone far removed from our real lives, someone we know only through the parallel universe of television and the movies.

Of course, I knew girls who, even at twelve, seemed to have gone straight from jump-rope games to French kissing with barely a heartbeat separating the two. I never thought any of those girls had any reason to pay much attention to the Fabians, David Cassidys, Corey Haims, or James van der Beeks of their times. There's a reason why our grandmas referred to them as "fast."

But those other girls, the ones whose parents wouldn't let them date until they were considerably older than twelve or who felt no natural attraction to the geeky preteen boys that inhabited their world, those are the girls I wonder about. No amount of strict parenting or religious guilt-tripping can stop us from the perfectly natural process of falling in love. What proportion of those girls fall in love for the first time with someone as safely inaccessible as a teen idol?

I only ever dared to ask one other girl in those days. If I recall, her name was Angie. I saw her only on the rarest occasions. She was the cousin of Joanne, the daughter of one of my mother's friends. I was only marginally friendly with Joanne because she was a couple of years older than me. Also, she was kind of mean. She loved reminding me that I was "just a baby" and would never understand anything.

Angie was about the same age as Joanne, but she was a much nicer girl. Also, she lived far, far away from the Bronx, all the way the hell out in Brooklyn somewhere, so there was

> *"Did you ever fall in love with somebody from TV?" I asked Angie when Joanne had stepped away.*
> *To my great relief, Angie didn't look at me like I was yet another dorky kid in her already dork-filled universe.*

no danger of her broadening my circle of ridicule by sharing what I thought I was about to reveal about myself to any of my friends at school. Even if Angie told Joanne, the risk was minimal; Joanne and I went to different schools.

"Did you ever fall in love with somebody from TV?" I asked Angie when Joanne had stepped away.

To my great relief, Angie didn't look at me like I was yet another dorky kid in her already dork-filled universe. In fact, she looked absolutely relieved herself. "*Yes!*" she said as she leaned in closer to me. She seemed to deflate somehow when she let out that response, but she was happy, smiling. It was as if she had been waiting for eons to let go of that breath, for someone to ask her this question specifically.

I scooted over to sit closer to her. "Who?" I asked, while silently I prayed, "Don't let her say David. Don't let her say David."

"Well, this is really embarrassing because I know it's weird, but I'm totally in love with Speed Racer."

I'm sure my reaction was written nakedly all over my young face. "The cartoon?" I asked incredulously.

"I know. It's weird, right? But I can't help it! I love him!"

There's a world of difference between a twelve-year-old girl and a fourteen-year-old one. Just a few moments before, I wasn't even sure a cool and pretty high school girl like Angie would even entertain the notion of speaking to me, let alone share the intimate details of her most desperately secret love life. I stared at her, probably too long. "Oh," I said at last.

"What about you?" There was such sweetness in her eyes and something like hope imprinted on her face that it almost broke my heart. Was there something wrong with her? Something I hadn't noticed or didn't know? Had she been dropped on her head as a baby? Is that why she lived in Brooklyn and only came to visit once or twice a year?

"No," I lied. "There's nobody like that I like. I was just wondering."

Angie's face fell. Even though I did, in fact, think she was weird, I didn't want her to feel badly because of it. "But that Speed Racer, well . . . yeah. He is kind of cute. I can see why you like him. And Astro Boy, too. Right?"

Angie perked right up. "*Astro Boy*? But he's just . . . a *boy*! And a *robot*!" It was then that she laughed and rolled her eyes at me, like she was talking to a big dumb baby after all. "Speed is a *man*," she said and smiled knowingly.

Right.

At least this was one chick I wouldn't have to worry about stealing my David.

However many of us start out falling in love with prime-time and matinee idols, I think it's a pretty safe bet that most of us do, in fact, move on and learn to have real relationships with actual flesh-and-blood human beings. And however unrequited those first strange loves are, by reality's necessity or just plain bad luck, we can all look forward to at least one more of those heartbreaks at some point along the way. If we're lucky, it'll be just the one.

Of course, not all imaginary love affairs begin and end in preadolescence, nor are they the exclusive domain of overprotected starstruck girls who may or may not have been dropped on their heads as babies. Even gainfully employed grown men have been known to suffer bouts of temporary insanity when in the grips of celebrity love.

A few years ago, famous *American Idol* judge Paula Abdul paid a routine visit to her gynecologist's office, who asked her to leave a urine specimen with the receptionist. The container soon went missing. They later discovered that one of the doctor's own staff,

> *Sometimes celebrities lust madly after each other and are every bit as unattainable to themselves as they are to us.*

who happened to be madly in love with Paula, stole the little plastic cup and its contents to keep as a souvenir. The man was fired as soon as he was identified as the culprit, but as far as we know, he may still be in possession of his golden trophy.

A passion for celebrities and the ensuing agony of unrequited love are also not limited to the antics of obsessed fans with no respect for boundaries. Sometimes celebrities lust madly after each other and are every bit as unattainable to themselves as they are to us.

Ernest Hemingway fell as hard for Marlene Dietrich as had most anyone who had ever paid 10 cents to see the stunning beauty on the silver screen. Unlike those fans, however,

Hemingway was actually lucky enough to meet her. They both happened to be headed back to America on the same French ocean liner in 1934.

"The Kraut," as Hemingway playfully referred to his elusive beloved, didn't exactly shun him in the same way she might have dismissed any other poor love-sick schmo, but I'm sure his pet name for her didn't help matters, either. Nevertheless, they struck up a friendship of sorts and maintained a correspondence over a period of many years—until, that is, he blew his own brains out in 1961.

In one of the many letters and telegrams recently released by the Kennedy Library in Boston, Hemingway once asked Marlene, "What do you really want to do for a life work? Break everybody's heart for a dime? You could always break mine for a nickel, and I'd bring the nickel."

Such a gift for words.

In trying to explain to a friend why they never actually consummated their relationship, Hemingway said, "Those times when I was out of love, the Kraut was deep in some romantic tribulation, and on those occasions when Dietrich was on the surface and swimming about with those marvelously seeking eyes, I was submerged." As he put it, they were the victims of "unsynchronized passion."

In the world of us lowly mortals, the phrase that comes to mind is, "she just wasn't that into you."

Marlene, for all her legendary aloofness, was nonetheless quite the flirty bird herself. She did, in fact, reach a point in their transcontinental correspondence at which she found herself having to admit that she had feelings for him, too. "I read your letters over and over and speak of you with a few chosen men."

I'm sure that conjured up all sorts of green-tinged images in Hemingway's head. Unrequited love is funny that way.

I suspect the reason why some of us fall in love with someone as utterly inaccessible as a movie star or, for that matter, a cartoon character, has a lot to do with the notion that, by their very distance from the tangibility of our own reality, they can't hurt us. We can surrender completely to the kind of unbridled passion they inspire in us, and we can actually enjoy how good it feels to be crazy in love without having to fear or look for any possible signs of rejection.

Eventually, though, the unavoidable anvil of unrequited love comes crashing out of the sky. We either step aside just in time and walk away, a little or a lot shaken from the experience but still alive, or we're totally crushed under the weight of it, in which case we are walked away by the authorities, either in handcuffs or a straitjacket.

Interestingly, a middle ground seems to have opened up between the two worlds, the one in which we fall in love with real people and brace our egos for the inevitable bumps and bruises yet to come, and the world in which we fall in love with those who live in the alternate reality of celebritydom and imagination.

Among other things, the phenomenon known as transformation fetish (TF) allows people to explore their romantic and/or sexual aspirations with one foot planted, however shakily, in each world.

By all accounts, TF is a very broad term covering all manner of fantasy relationships and sexual encounters. People who are routinely dumped into TF's various subgroups and related categories spend an inordinate amount of time debating over who actually qualifies for membership and who's just plain weird. I won't attempt to engage in the debate. It's all fascinating to me.

The core characteristic of TF, if there is one, is that it involves being captivated by, attracted to, and/or sexually aroused by the process of transformation itself—people turning into other people (like celebrities), other beings (like animals, spirits, or aliens), or other things (like panty hose or dishwashing liquid).

> *"She was just another guy after all," Todd later told me with a sad sort of sigh. "I wish I'd never seen her that way."*

Many years ago, I went with a group of coworkers to a cabaret after work one Friday night. We were led there by our friend, Todd, who happened to be madly in love with one of the performers, a female impersonator who looked eerily more like Sigourney Weaver than Sigourney herself, despite the fact that she lip-synched to songs by Cher, that she was (at least biologically) a man, and that Todd was gay and most often attracted to big, brawny macho types like firemen and construction workers. We had the most wonderful time that night, but I must say that it was, without question, the most confusing four hours of my life.

Todd had no real interest in the performer in his/her natural state. It was only as Sigourney Weaver that she became utterly irresistible to him. Back then, I didn't know there was such a thing as transformation fetish, but I would guess now that this might have been one form of it.

For a long time Todd tried unsuccessfully to get the make-believe Sigourney to fall in love with him. Alas, in the end, she was no more accessible to him than the real Sigourney would have been. His crush finally ended when he made friends with the cabaret owner, a big brawny guy, and was allowed to visit the make-believe Sigourney backstage one night. It was very late, after the show, and the wig and makeup had already come off. "She was just another guy after all," Todd later told me with a sad sort of sigh. "I wish I'd never seen her that way."

I'd love to be able to say he fared better with the club owner, but that turned out to be another dream stomped to dust, too. Poor Todd. He was such a nice guy.

I still wonder if he ever found his perfect match, and in what shape or form that love finally arrived. With Todd, it was hard to tell.

It would never have occurred to me that a person could become attracted to or aroused by watching someone turn into butter. Literally.

I don't know why I keep getting surprised by these things. By now I should know better. But every time I think I've seen and heard it all, a whole new subculture emerges and knocks my socks off all over again.

This other variation of TF, the one in which people are turned on by watching someone become some*thing* versus some*one* else, is by necessity an event that takes place mostly in the imagination. Fans of this form of TF are aided in their explorations by very imaginative (if disturbing) artwork and computer animations. There is no costume that can help transform a human being into an ice cold can of Diet Coke or a glob of shaving cream, but watching it happen on a computer screen is plenty for most of these folks.

The only possible exception is yet another variation on the variation, something called agalmatophilia. This phenomenon refers to feeling love for or sexual attraction to a statue, doll, mannequin, or other object that resembles the human form in some way.

It's a lot easier for two TF fans to role-play an agalmatophilic moment. One of them would just have to lie very, very still when he or she is finished "transforming" into a mannequin or sculpture. I suppose it would help if the one turning into the statue then "freezes" in just the right pose to allow for the logistics of some kind of sexual encounter.

Some agalmatophiles, of course, don't bother with the human partner at all. They can just go out and hump a statue.

Men who love big beautiful women are not uncommon, even in a society such as our own, obsessed with holding up near-death supermodels as the gold standard for female beauty. In some countries, including the United States (albeit to a lesser degree, generally speaking), a woman's voluptuous curves, beefy legs, and beach-ball-like buttocks can send some men happily into fits of lustful ecstasy. Throughout Latin America, both men and women are very quick to assert, "Bone is for the dog. Meat is for the man."

Some years ago, I knew a woman from Africa's Cote d'Ivoire who once told me the happiest moment of her life was when she stepped on the scale and saw that she had gained back the eighty-five pounds she had lost during a long illness. In her country, the larger a woman is, the more prosperous her family is perceived to be. To these same women, the most desirable men, the ones they would judge as hardworking and exceedingly good providers, are all as thin as reeds. A perfect marriage, then, is one composed of a gigantic well-fed wife and her industrious beanpole of a husband.

We don't have to travel very far, however, to find ordinary normal-looking men obsessed with extraordinarily large women. Not just big beautiful women, but actual towering giants.

I saw a photograph that so disturbed me that I seriously began to question my commitment to becoming the arch nemesis of the Old Aunts. "This had to be Photoshopped," I thought. Now I'm not so sure.

Most of the picture was taken up by what I first thought was a sumo wrestler suspended in midair but then realized was a naked woman. She was hoisted a few feet above the floor by a system of ropes and pulleys, spread-eagle and with a somewhat noncommittal look on her face. She was staring straight at the camera. A skinny little man was sitting below her with his legs sprawled out on the floor. His whole head was inside her vagina.

His entire head.

The one above his shoulders.

Medical textbooks tell us that the female sex organ is a cunningly flexible little orifice, capable of enveloping itself snugly around the circumference of an object as thin as a swizzle stick or expelling something as large as a twelve-pound baby. So I suppose anything's possible.

I couldn't tell from that picture, though, whether that woman was exceedingly large, whether the man was unusually small, or whether he had gone in there hooked up to an oxygen tank.

This particular fetish is called macrophilia—the love of big things. It did not surprise me to learn that almost all macrophiles are men. I can't imagine many women wanting to go prospecting in a similar fashion in the only possible body cavity a man can offer for such a purpose. But who can say for sure.

For some macrophiles, their feelings of love and/or sexual pleasure are derived from being infantilized. Their transformation fetish is about being miniaturized in some way. They seek out enormous motherlike creatures who can carry them around the house, cradle them like babies, powder and diaper their asses, pretend to breast-feed them, and spank them when they're naughty.

For others the fetish is entirely about being crushed like a bug under the feet or shoes of a woman as big as a skyscraper, or squished like something gooey between her enormous toes. Women of such height are a rather scarce commodity, but the Internet provides plenty of imaginatively drawn images and role-playing virtual worlds in which to explore these particular TF fantasies.

Many men who purport to be macrophiles say their emergence as such began rather early in life, even before adolescence. Stories such as *Gulliver's Travels* and movies like *Godzilla, King Kong,* and *Attack of the 50-Foot Woman* started them wondering what life would be like in a lilliputian world and later influenced the paths their sexual predilections would take. For some gay macrophiles, G.I. Joe and Ken dolls figure prominently in their repertoire of playtime accessories.

One of the many variations on this macrophilic theme is called vorarephilia—the desire to be consumed or devoured by a giant, like a snack. If such a thing were possible, it would have to be a one-time pleasure. In the virtual world, it's a repeatable indulgence.

The laws of physics tell us that for every action there is an equal and opposite reaction. If there are macrophiles living and working among us—and I assure you, there are—the world must also make room for the microphiles who love them back. As the name would imply, a microphile is a big person who loves tiny people or human-like creatures. A microphile could also be an average-size person with fantasies of being transformed into something gigantic enough to dwarf the normal-size world.

> *The laws of physics tell us that for every action there is an equal and opposite reaction. If there are macrophiles living and working among us—and I assure you, there are—the world must also make room for the microphiles who love them back.*

And wherever there is a niche market, there's someone making a profit.

There are many unusually large women who happily hire themselves out to play the role of overbearing perverted mother and/or looming dominatrix and make quite a decent living at it. There is also a plethora of graphic artists and digital imaging experts who run lucrative businesses feeding the fantasy worlds many macro- and microphiles must inhabit by necessity.

I've decided I'm just going to be glad everybody's found a way to be happy.

There is a great deal of debate—often very heated—currently taking place among fans of TF and the "furries," people who like to dress up and have sex as animals or plush toys.

Some furries are happy to claim TF as their own personal fetish. Others resent the very notion, stating that it's not about the transformation, but the act of *being* something else that gives them pleasure and better represents their true inner selves. Still others claim that furrydom has nothing to do with yiffing (their word for having sex); it's all about embracing an alternate identity, in particular one that is chaste and wholesome. The concept of fetishism itself is offensive to certain furries who live otherwise respectable lives, like the ones who get married and have kittens (or puppies or cubs or whatever their legally sanctioned yiffing produces).

Intentionally or not, it appears the furries are doing a fine job of mimicking both the animal kingdom and the world of upright humans. Not only are they waging war against their natural enemies (people who are not furries), but there's a tremendous amount of fighting among themselves regarding the actual composition of their own community.

For some furries, clipping a tail to the back belt loop of their pants and maybe donning a pair of bunny ears is quite enough of a transformation to achieve the desired effect. For others, nothing but the full monty will do.

Not surprisingly, there are many married furries. Most often, a nonfurry becomes a convert after discovering that the person who has stolen his or her heart has an alternate identity.

There's a woman who calls herself Kowe Chobe who describes her furry incarnation as a "black pantherwolf." She apparently fancies herself the product of interspecies breeding. She had been living as a furry for many years when she met her husband. Several months into their marriage, he assumed his own furry identity as a "werret," some kind of wolf-ferret. A year into their marriage, they were expecting their first "little fur."[6]

Furry Mouse, a veteran member of an online furry community, welcomed Kowe and her husband with a friendly warning: "Be wary of gay furs who claim to be able to 'change' your husband."

By most accounts, an unusually high percentage of furries are gay. I'm sure we can all draw any number of inappropriate conclusions and vivid mental images about that, but something tells me this isn't a group we'd like coming after us with fantasies of revenge. I can easily imagine sharp teeth and spring-loaded claws being part of the standard accoutrements

---

[6] Gag.

for some of the more committed afi-
cionados. More significantly, homosexuality, in whatever proportion it
may exist in this group, seems the
least interesting of their quirks.
I mean, think about it: two or
more people dressed as rac-
coons and porcupines, maybe
even tigers and bears, getting
it on doggy-style in the forest or somebody's basement
rec room . . . does it really
matter which one is the
wife?

There are many asex-
ual furries who simply feel
a greater affinity with animals
than with people. Others believe
that they are animals trapped in human bodies.
A few argue that the world is, very possibly, full of furries
who may not yet be aware that that feeling of being "different" is their inner furryness yearning to break free of whatever closet or hollow tree trunk that keeps them from living
the lives they were meant to experience.

Like I said, there's a lot of disagreement among the
ranks.

One trait that all furries do seem to share is the taking of
an evocative name to complete their animal identities. The
chairman of the All Fur Fun Convention held in Spokane,

Washington, in 2007, for example, is a registered orthodontics technician who calls himself Moorcat when he is not helping to adjust the wires on some poor kid's braces. The head of security at that same convention was, appropriately, a "wolf" named Lupercus.

Furry attire is a huge international business in this community that's growing every day. Companies like Irene Corey Design Associates and Sugar's Mascot Costumes specialize in costumes like the ones worn by sports team mascots and television "fursonalities" (their word) like Barney. Most costume makers also offer specialty alterations for furries seeking unique anatomical accommodations. A custom-made suit can cost several thousand dollars.

A furry named Crssa Fox sadly had to put her elaborately made vixen costume up for sale on Furbid.com (eBay for furries) so she could complete the down payment on the house she wanted to buy. She says of her beloved vulpine ensemble, "She's gently used, only been worn for FWA [Furry Weekend Atlanta] and Megaplex [the Jacksonville, Florida, furry convention], as well as the Easter Egg hunt at church. And that's ALL!"

I guess that means her fox suit's trapdoor remains virginal. I would love to know what her fellow church members thought of her appearance as the Easter Fox, though.

And what subculture would be complete without its own retinue of perverts and detractors? There are, in fact, furries on the fringes who scare and/or disgust the hell out of the normal furries. There is also no shortage of critics.

Some of the so-called pervert furries not only like to dress up as their favorite animal, but they take great pleasure in yiffing inanimate furries, like teddy bears.

My first reaction upon learning this was, "Now that's just not right." But then I remembered that I'm working very hard not to become an Old Aunt, so I tried to think about it a different way: "The teddy bear is just a foam-stuffed piece of cloth with buttons for eyes and a plastic triangle for a nose. It's not a real bear."

That didn't work. It still seems pretty creepy.

There are many antifurry Web sites engaged in all manner of outrage and ridicule, two in particular that I found very funny. The one called GodHatesFurries.com is intentionally funny. The site's owner hardly has to do any work at all to make that happen; the hate mail alone is hysterical. The other Web site is TrueChristian.com. That one should win some kind of award. It's the antithesis of informed thought.

One message posted on Godhatesfurries.com was from an incensed critter named Christian Kimmey. My guess is that he wasn't wearing his costume at the time he wrote the e-mail because he didn't use his furry name; either that or the furry version of himself can't type. The subject of the message was, "Salutations from an intellectual." The letter begins, "What the fuck is your problem?!?!?" Mr. Kimmey then proceeds to quote Jesus and "other holy documents" in his attempt to enlighten the Webmaster and restore respectability to his community.

The other Web site, TrueChristian.com, has devoted a considerable amount of space to explaining the furry movement to the normal people. Pastor Jim Nicholls writes, "Through my travels on the Internet I've found many female furries with . . . penises. No I'm not kidding, this furry thing is tied into a lot of cross-dressed and transsexuals. Most furries are essentially hermaphrodites or homosexuals. The entire furry movement generally is revolved around sex and sex with animals. It's basically the typical tree hugging hippie fetish of today."

> *Among those at whom the good reverend points his True Christian finger are "some really extremist liberals" (a group into which he lumps all members of PETA), "various science fiction geeks," vegans, and other "major perverts."*

Among those at whom the good reverend points his True Christian finger are "some really extremist liberals" (a group into which he lumps all members of PETA), "various science fiction geeks," vegans, and other "major perverts."

I wonder who plays the Easter Bunny at Pastor Nicholls's church.

No discussion of furries would be complete without at least a mention of those who fantasize and obsess over Disney characters, in particular the ones that resemble animals.

For as long as Disney has been hiring people to wear Goofy heads and Donald Duck tail feathers, rumors have abounded regarding the secret lives of the people behind the masks. Orgies, X-rated reenactments of the G-rated movies, even Disney "snuff" films are said to have been taking place or circulating for decades.

Some of the people who eagerly don their favorite Disney characters' costumes and assume their personae, whether they get paid for it or not, claim to be true furries. Some even brag about the never-in-short-supply attentions of their very own Disney groupies. The Walt Disney Corporation frowns upon this sort of thing, of course, but that has never put a damper on the goings-on.

But even beyond the most frayed fringes of the Magic Kingdom's employee base and the strange little twists the furries have given to Disneymania, there is an unbelievably fertile cartoon porn industry feeding the fantasies of people who fell in love with these characters as children, and whose sexual awakening somehow merged with what these images represented to them.

Dan Savage, a columnist who writes for the *Metro Times* in Detroit, has an interesting theory about furries. He says, "After being exposed to [Disney's] images of cuddly, safe, saucer-eyed, anthropomorphized animals throughout their childhoods, during puberty these same kids had sex presented to them as something deadly and dangerous . . . Is it any wonder that a tiny percentage of this Disney/abstinence generation came to fetishize the safe and cuddly stuffed animals of their childhoods?"

I like this theory as a possible explanation for the latest generation of furries, the ones who grew up in the last couple of decades and in particular those with Disney fixations, but something tells me furries have been around much, much longer than that.

Werewolf legends have been around for centuries, mostly scaring people half to death, but I bet turning a few of them on along the way as well. And even before that, the Greeks invented Pan, a flute-playing, cloven-hooved half-man half-beast who loved orgies more than life itself.

I'm sure Lon Chaney as the Wolfman inspired more than a few secret bedroom fantasies in the 1940s. I know for a fact that Frank Langella as Dracula drove women wild in the 1970s, although perhaps not as many when he turned into a bat. However, I'm no longer inclined to rule out the possibility that somebody somewhere, in some darkened movie house or drive-in theater, found that bat sexy, and maybe even felt the first timorous stirrings of a strange new imaginary romance beginning to bloom.

Believing one has fallen deeply and seriously in love with a movie star or teen idol may, unfortunately, seem weird and pathetic to people who have never experienced such a phenomenon. If the object of one's affection happens to be an actual object, that perception of weirdness can be greatly intensified. Feeling love for or sexual attraction to a cartoon character or a fake animal, no matter how cute, sexy, or cuddly it may be depicted, will simply leave some people speechless. And maybe that's exactly as it should be.

CHAPTER SIX

Speaking in Tongues

> I haven't spoken
> to my wife in years.
> I didn't want to
> INTERRUPT HER.
>
> —RODNEY DANGERFIELD

"What do men want, really?" I asked my dear friend Ernie, the most unapologetically macho man I know.

"Men want women who will leave them alone," he explained, as if this were self-evident.

Ordinarily, I'd feel perfectly justified in smacking the crap out of someone who answered a legitimate question so rudely. But I've known Ernie long enough to know that there's often a bit of interesting logic behind his most outrageous opinions. That's why I chose to ask him this particular question, and not some sensitive guy who would fill my head with a bunch of dumb platitudes. I knew I could trust him to tell me the truth.

"What do you mean, leave you alone?"

"It's simple. Men are simple. It's like this: We need to

be out in the world doing things that are important to us—working, building things, killing stuff. It's encoded in our DNA. It's what we do. But women don't get that. Instead, they get all crazy and complain that we don't spend any time with them."

"So why do men get married?"

He pouted, scratched himself, and responded, "What does that have to do with anything?"

It's an absolute mystery to me that men and women can actually communicate effectively enough to make it past a third date. As soon as we get comfortable with each other, we begin to speak completely different languages.

> *When a man says something like, "I want to spend the rest of my life with you," what she hears is, "I want to spend time with you, every day, until one of us drops dead." This makes her happy.*

Communication in the beginning of a relationship is no real mystery. Those first few weeks, we're both driven insane by hormone surges, giddy optimism, unacknowledged desperation, drooling lust, mad obsession, the relief and horror of recognizing our own dumb luck, the specter of childhood fears lurking in shadowy corners, and the unimaginable joy of discovering that someone else in the world finds us almost as beautiful and fascinating as we find ourselves.

This we call "love in full bloom." It lasts about a month.

Once the hormones settle down and the mutual fascination subsides, we slowly begin to gather the strewn bits and pieces of our regular lives and try to put things more or less back into some kind of order. We then attempt to communicate in normal, everyday language and suddenly realize that we have no idea what the other person is saying.

Here's an excerpt from a conversation I once had with my own dearly beloved. We'd been together about three months at the time:

Me: I hate my boss.
Him: You want me to kill him?
Me: What? No! I'm just telling you! I'm just talking!
Him: Talking? Why?

Conversely, when a man speaks in what he thinks is perfectly clear language, it is she who will invariably find herself stuck in a mire of utter confusion. When a man says something like, "I want to spend the rest of my life with you," what she hears is, "I want to spend *time* with you, *every day,* until one of us drops *dead.*" This makes her happy.

The key phrase—"spending time"—strikes abject terror into the hearts of most men. To women, it encompasses all of life itself, including but not limited to: eating meals, complaining about work, raising a family, paying bills, folding laundry, making each other laugh, deciding what to have for dinner, inventing new ways to have foreplay, planning vacations, watching television, entertaining the in-laws, picking out wallpaper, barbecuing with the neighbors, figuring out the meaning of life, washing the car, and occasionally agreeing to watch each other's movies without wondering out loud whether one has married a total moron—or worse—a latent homicidal maniac.

If men knew that this is what women really hear, they would never again utter the words, "I want to spend the rest of my life with you." Not ever again.

Interestingly, sometimes it's this very inability to communicate in the same language that actually conspires to bring a couple together. My cousin Robert told me a story that proves this to be true.

Robert was a regular at a club called the Lemon Tree in Forest Hills, Queens, during the wild and woolly days of disco. Robert never struck me as quite the disco type, so the mental image this conjured in my mind as he was telling me this story was a little frightening. I could see it much too clearly: platform shoes, bell bottoms, gigantic hair, paisley shirt covered in dizzying swirls of explosive psychedelic patterns . . . He probably didn't look anything like that, but nothing will ever get that image out of my head now.

"I went there all the time," he said. "And then one night, I saw her: Disco Girl."

"Did she see you?" I asked, still imagining him in his dancing-machine getup and trying very hard to convince myself that I myself never danced with a guy in a club who looked like that.

"I'm trying to tell you a story," he said.

"Were you wearing paisley?"

"You're killing me."

"Sorry. Go on."

"So I see Disco Girl and decide to make my move—that's what we called it in those days. I asked her to dance, she put her purse on the bar, and off we went."

"Wait a minute," I interrupted again, "It's 1970s New York City. You meet some chick in a club and she leaves her purse on the bar, unattended, so she can go dance with you, a stranger? What was she, from Upstate?"

"It was a pretty safe place. And it was Queens, for crying out loud."

"Oh. Okay."

When they returned, the purse was gone.

Robert the Lemon Tree Regular had become friendly with the club owner over time, so he immediately went looking for him to tell him what had happened. To Robert's great surprise, the club owner had an entire collection of purses he had confiscated from a thief working the bar that night. Robert went back for Disco Girl and led her to the stash, where she immediately spotted her black Coach bag. Bag and Disco Girl were happily reunited, and Robert the Disco King escorted them both back to the bar.

A strange look soon crept over Disco Girl's face. She stared at Robert darkly—almost menacingly—for a long time. Finally, she said, "Oh, I see how this works. You and the club owner are in cahoots. You ask me to dance, I leave my purse, somebody from the club swipes my bag and puts it in the lost and found box like it was 'lost.' I panic, you disappear, you come back ten seconds later like you're a hero, and the club owner magically produces my purse. So now it's like I 'owe' you, right? This is how you get women to sleep with you?"

Robert looked at her, thunderstruck. "Wow," he thought. "This woman thinks I'm brilliant!"

He did his best to convince her that there was no collusion between him and the club owner. "I'm really not that clever," he told her honestly, "but I'm flattered you think I'm bright enough to concoct such a plan."

Apparently, it was this sweet moment of self-deprecation that won her over. And so began a relationship that lasted at least six months, a long time indeed in those heady days of disco.

It would appear that Mother Nature doesn't really care whether or not we speak the same language. All she wants is to create opportunities for reproduction. Even the occasional outrageous misunderstanding can lead some couples to play right into the plan. Any old series of wildly convoluted conversations and misinterpretations can work just as brilliantly as the plain old truth.

Yet, despite Mother Nature's indifference and this apparent inability of men and women to speak the same language, there are marriages whose longevity threatens to stretch out into infinity.

I don't believe that people who have been married for more than a couple of decades have learned to communicate any better than couples who have just begun their respective journeys together. I think the longer-lived ones simply figured out early on that you just can't listen too closely to what the love of your life is saying.

Take, for example, Liu Yang-Wan and her husband, Liu Yung-Yang, who were married in Taiwan in 1917. She was 103 years old when the photographer showed up on the occasion of the couple's eighty-sixth wedding anniversary in 2003. Their picture was reproduced in newspapers and magazines the world over. Liu Yang-Wan looked like she was sound asleep, possibly dead. Her husband held her hand and smiled, sort of. Looking at them, I became convinced this was not a woman who had been hanging on her husband's every word for eighty-six years. For his part, and as well as he was able, Liu Yung-Yang was beside himself with joy.

The same was true for Percy Arrowsmith and his dearly beloved, Florence, who celebrated their eightieth wedding anniversary at their home in Hereford, England, in 2005. Florence, God bless her, appeared much more alert than Liu Yang-Wan in her photograph, though she squinted at the camera in a way that suggested she was either really pissed off or confused about all the fuss. Percy, like his Taiwanese counterpart, wore a crooked little smile.

A British reporter asked Percy what he thought the secret might be to sustaining such a remarkably long marriage. Percy affirmed that it all comes down to two little words: "Yes, dear."

I bet Percy hasn't heard a word Flo has said since 1923. But it looks like he never told her to shut up, either, and this seems to have worked remarkably well for them both.

My own parents, who first met back when Elvis was skinny, have one of those marriages that seem to support the theory that you can only listen to your beloved with no more than half an ear. Here's a transcript of an actual conversation I once heard them have:

Mom: Oh, no! We're out of milk!
Dad: Hmm?
Mom: We're out of milk.
Dad: Hmm?
Mom: We have to go to the store. To get some milk.
Dad: Hmm?
Mom: We need milk.
Dad: Hmm?
Mom: We're out of milk.
Dad: Hmm?
Mom (looking at Dad): Oh, my God! Did you go outside today wearing that?
Dad: Hmm?

The whole time, Dad was watching a ball game. He got up from his chair a few hours later and said to no one in particular, "Oh-oh! We're out of milk!"

A day or so later, my nephew, Alex, came by for a visit. Here's the conversation he had with my mother:

Mom: Alex! Where are your shoes?
Alex: Hmm?
Mom: Your shoes.
Alex: Hmm?

Mom: We have to put on your shoes.
Alex: Hmm?
Mom: Where did you leave your shoes?
Alex: Hmm?

Holy cow, I thought. This little boy thinks this is how people talk to each other!

At first I worried that Alex had spent way too much of his babyhood and toddlerdom at my parents' house, and that this is what he had learned about communication between men and women. But after some consideration, I realized that, if my theory is correct, Alex and whomever he marries will probably be together a hundred years—especially if the love of his life isn't too fussy about getting a real answer to any of her questions.

There's a Philadelphia couple who may have started things off on exactly the right foot when they began their engagement by taking a month-long vow of silence.

Jennifer Farina and Ryan Donlon took part in the My M&Ms Sweet Silence challenge in June 2007. For every day in a span of thirty-one days that the couple succeeded in keeping mum, the candy company would give them $1,000. Cameras were set up in their home to capture any surreptitious attempts at ventriloquism.

The couple arranged to have about nine thousand M&Ms imprinted with messages they could use to communicate nonverbally. They also made up rules for having color-coded exchanges; the red M&Ms were for expressing anger and moments of craziness, and the pink ones were to be used in lieu of whispering sweet nothings.

Jennifer and Ryan won the challenge. The Mars candy company, which owns M&Ms, awarded them $31,000 for living together without speaking to each other. The couple planned to use the money to pay for their dream wedding.

When they were finally allowed to speak, Ryan asked his bride-to-be, "Have you seen my brown shoes?"

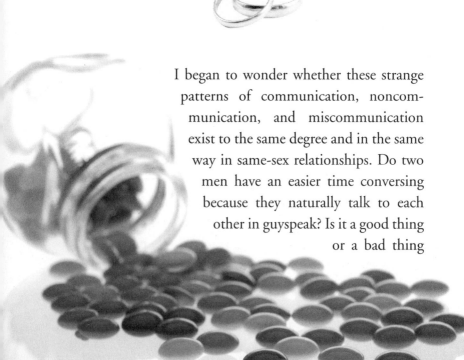

I began to wonder whether these strange patterns of communication, noncommunication, and miscommunication exist to the same degree and in the same way in same-sex relationships. Do two men have an easier time conversing because they naturally talk to each other in guyspeak? Is it a good thing or a bad thing when two women are free to take each other literally, and actually listen to and remember every word that's ever uttered between them?

I decided to ask my dear friend, Matt, who lets me ask him any dumb thing I want and always loves me anyway. "Mattie," I said, "What does it mean when a gay man grunts?"

"Oh, honey . . ."

"Well, now, hold on a second," I said before he could drag me all too gleefully into some even more mysterious corner of the universe. "I mean 'grunt' as in, 'there's your answer.' Or don't you do that?"

By the look on Matt's face, I could tell I was being a little vague, even for Matt, who is very smart, so I tried to explain it better: "You see, when a guy grunts in response to something his wife or girlfriend is saying, it can mean any number of things. It can mean, 'Yes,' it can mean, 'No,' it can mean, 'I don't care,' it can mean, 'Uh-oh, she's talking again,' or 'Talk to me after the game. I can't listen to this right now. Or ever.'"

"Unnmgh," Matt grunted.

"Yeah. Like that. What does that mean?"

"Well, right now, it means, 'I see. I understand.'"

"Do you and Rob grunt in response to each other's questions?"

"Oh, no," Matt responded unequivocally. "Rob is much too cultured for that. But I've known others. After those first three months, the longest sentence you can get out of them most days is, 'Unnmgh.'"

Three months, Matt said. Not thirty days. I made a mental note of that.

"Hmmm," I said. "Has Rob ever offered to kill your boss for you, like after you've had a bad day at work?"

Matt thought about this for a second. "Well, you know, just the other day, I was trying to tell him about this coworker who was totally making my life miserable, and Rob says to me, 'Oh, honey, we both know that woman is awful. Just have another glass of wine and forget about it.' I was *devastated*. All I wanted to do was talk about it for ten or twelve hours. You understand that, right?"

"Absolutely."

It made me happy, somehow, to know this. Not that I was glad Matt didn't get what he needed from that aborted conversation, but I understood what he meant about just wanting to talk. I also felt a little less crazy for wanting to complain about my stupid boss without having my boyfriend offer to kill him.

"You want to know the real difference between men and women?" Matt asked. Of course I wanted to know. "When two men argue, it's a fight to the death. Neither one of us will ever back down or give an inch. That has nothing to do with being gay or straight. It has everything to do with being a red-blooded American male. We're just not raised to back down from a fight. And this is where women have all the power. Even when they know they're right, women will, at some point, back down from an argument, if only to stop the fighting. And that's how they win. Knowing they're right is enough. That's how they're more powerful than men."

I thought about all the times I was willing to fight to the death for my argument, and all the times I'd chosen to walk away, right or wrong, in a huff, or simply too tired or bored to keep trying to beat some dumb point into my beloved's thick skull. Walking away was the hands-down winner. Until this moment, though, I had never considered it might be a sign of power. I simply took it as proof that the person trying to argue with me "to the death" was a jackass.

"But here's where women lose me," Matt continued. "They withhold sex when they're angry. Men will *never* withhold sex from each other. That just makes no sense to us. No matter how hurt or angry we are, who's wrong, who's right, or who's crazy, we will *never* withhold sex. Hell, we'll even have sex *while* we're fighting, and then continue the fight later if we have to."

> *"Women withhold sex when they're angry. Men will never withhold sex from each other. That just makes no sense to us."*

"Unnmgh," I grunted.

I wasn't sure there was anything else I could say.

I still wondered about communication in female couples. So I asked my friend Annie, who also lets me ask her any dumb thing I want and only rarely rolls her eyes at me.

"Well, you know the old joke about lesbians," she began.

"Which one?"

Her eyes narrowed. I grinned idiotically.

"The one that goes, 'What does a lesbian bring to the second date?'" Annie prompted.

"A U-Haul," I answered dutifully.

"Well, it's true," she said. "Most of the time. Well, no, not most. Some of the time. When we're in our twenties. And sometimes our thirties. Not so much in our forties. But yes. We're the biggest part of U-Haul's customer base."

I think she was trying to make a joke, but I wasn't sure. I decided I'd ask one of my other friends later.

"Our communication problems tend to appear out of nowhere and then either resolve or explode just as quickly," Annie continued. "I think it's because we want everything to happen *right now.* But it's more complicated than that."

"Of course it is," I answered knowingly. And then, dumbly, "What's complicated?"

"That the problem isn't only about whether or not we speak the same language. The problem is also that we talk too much. Everything has to be *processed.*"

"Of course," I said again. And then, "What do you mean?"

"It's like, whenever there's a conflict, first we process it all in our own heads. Then we process it as a couple. Then we process it with our other girlfriends. Sometimes the processing with each other gets way too loud and hurtful and somebody starts crying, so then we have to process *that*—in our own heads, with each other, and again with our girlfriends. Then sometimes we end up sleeping with one of the girlfriends, and next thing you know—U-Haul."

"*Really?*"

"No, silly. But yes. A lot more often than I like to admit. Especially when we're younger. As we get older, we tend to let a whole lot more shit slide. It's just too exhausting otherwise."

"Do you ever grunt?" I asked.

"Not without processing it," she said.

So what did I learn? When it comes to communicating with your beloved, the less said, the better.

CHAPTER SEVEN

Who's Counting?

> I'm the only man in the world with a marriage license made out "to whom it may concern."
>
> —MICKEY ROONEY

Grandmother Many-Names was one of those fabulous old Southern dames most of us only get to read about in overblown fiction or see in Tennessee Williams's plays. I was fortunate to have known her for a few short years when I was married to her second-favorite grandson.[7]

Many-Names had buried no fewer than four husbands but somehow ended up with six last names, some or all of which she used interchangeably at different times in her life and in no particular order. It seemed to depend on whether the current husband was dead or alive and where any one of them ranked in her memory or esteem at any given moment in time.

---

[7] Her most-favorite grandson was Chris the Doctor. She loved it when he visited. She would get palpitations and then brag to the rest of the family about how Chris had cured her. Unfortunately, my husband's own talents as a computer geek were of little use to an old lady. But she loved him, too. Just not as much.

She was as fearless about reinventing herself as she was about getting married. In addition to being a wife and matriarch, she embarked upon several different careers in her long and colorful life, not the least of which was becoming one of the first women ever to be elected to the North Carolina state senate.

It was, in fact, during her first run for office that a relatively rare moment of naïveté almost got the best of her. She went to a local print shop to have some campaign materials produced. "You need a slogan," the printer said to her. "For your buttons."

"Oh," she said, "You're right. What do you think they should say?"

The printer thought about it for a moment, then offered, "How about, 'Go All the Way with Mary Faye'?"

The man was clearly supporting the other candidate, a Republican.

Falling in love with the sound of that rhyme and a little out of touch with the parlance of the times, Many-Names ordered several hundred campaign buttons with that slogan. Very few of them actually made it into circulation, perhaps thanks to the keen young eyes of the hipper members of her campaign staff. She won the election anyway.

I had an opportunity to meet Many-Names's most-favorite grandson, Chris the Doctor, when he came down South one summer to introduce his fiancée to his mother's side of the family. My husband and I met them for dinner at a local restaurant, where the last vestiges of every illusion that I had married into a normal family vanished forever.

Many-Names insisted on paying for dinner, of course. As she signed the credit card slip, Chris noticed that her last name had changed yet again. "So now we're Hull again, I see."

"Yes. Hull is the name I use on my checks and for other personal business now that Sherwood's gone."

Mr. Sherwood was one scary old coot, I must say, about 173 years old when I first met him. The house he shared with Many-Names was full of the antiques he had collected through his travels around the world. He wore a white dress shirt and dark tie every day, and sat in a huge dusty armchair in a dim parlor, scowling and hunched over the cane planted between his long thin legs, with a cat every bit as suspicious and antisocial as its master at his feet. The heavy drapes over the windows had to be kept drawn because Mr. Sherwood was convinced there could be World War II Japanese soldiers hiding in the bougainvillea, lying in wait and biding their time, ready to recapture him in his own front yard.

> "You need a slogan . . . for your campaign buttons," the printer said to her. "How about, 'Go All the Way with Mary Faye'?"

Mr. Sherwood's last will and testament included a line that said something like, "And I'm taking the cat with me." So when he died, the family put the poor ancient feline out of its last bit of misery, cremated them both, and finally let the brilliant Carolina sun come pouring into that big old house for the first time in years.

"And then I took back Hull," said Many-Names.

Chris seemed to hesitate a moment before asking, but in the end couldn't help himself. "Hull was two or three husbands ago, wasn't he?"

"Yes. That was the one I married for love," she said and smiled. I think she may even have blushed.

My husband leaned over and whispered to me, "Hull was the first man to . . . um . . . curl her toes." I snapped my jaw shut almost as quickly as it had dropped onto my dessert plate. Then I put my eyes back into my head and tried hard to look like I was still listening politely.

"How would you know such a thing?!" I croaked in his ear.

"I'll tell you later."

Many-Names went on. "The others, well I married them for other reasons. For money, for social status, for company . . . Hull was the only one I married for love."

"Yeah, I remember that guy," Chris ventured gingerly, "But Grandmother . . . wasn't he, like . . . a Nazi?"

Rumor had it that one of Many-Names's many husbands was rather fond of the Confederate flag and a collector of the kind of historical paraphernalia that makes most of us queasy. I never met the man myself, so I can't attest to his character, but by all accounts he was a decent enough person . . . with a penchant for political incorrectness. And I knew Many-Names well enough to know that she would never have been deliberately involved with anyone who might have been purposefully evil.

So in response to her most-favorite grandson's query, she shot right back, as much in Mr. Hull's defense as in her own: "Well, *I* didn't know he was a Nazi! I thought he was a Democrat!"

I guess when you're in love, sometimes it's hard to tell the difference.

One of the questions this story raises in my mind is, what compels a person to marry over and over again?

Celebrities, of course, are typically as famous for the frequency and short duration of their marriages as they are for whatever else made them famous. The only ones who are truly unusual are the ones whose marriages last the longest, and those couples for whom divorce appears never to have been an option. Some of the most notable among these were Bob Hope and Dolores de Fina (sixty-nine years), Charlton Heston and Lydia Clarke (sixty-four years), Paul Newman and Joanne Woodward (fifty years), Kirk Douglas and Anne Buydens (fifty-four years and counting), and the youngsters of the group, Samuel L. Jackson and Latanya Richardson (thirty-five years and still going strong).

Then there are the others.

In the 1950s and 1960s, Zsa Zsa Gabor's name was the punch

line to practically every marriage joke told by every comedian of the times. Known more for her husbands than she ever was for her film career (honestly, can you name even two of her almost seventy movie and television roles without confusing her with her sister Eva?), Ms. Gabor has promised her eternal and undying love to no fewer than nine men. Only eight of them resulted in legal unions, though.

> *Just hours after they were married, Jean locked herself in the bathroom and wailed that she had made a terrible mistake. She later returned to the home of her former lover, actress Grace Diamond, and stayed with her.*

Her longest marriage is with her current husband, Frederic Prinz von Anhalt, who is neither a prince nor of royal lineage as far as anyone can tell, but he appears to like it when people think so. Her shortest marriage was to a Mexican film star named Felipe de Alba, which lasted almost a whole day in 1982 and was annulled the instant Zsa Zsa sobered up and remembered that she was still legally married to her seventh husband, Michael O'Hara. Interestingly, O'Hara was the attorney she had hired to divorce her sixth husband, Jack Ryan.

Of all her husbands, I'm most intrigued by actor George Sanders, to whom Zsa Zsa was married for five years. He himself was married four times. His last wife was Zsa Zsa's other sister, Magda. Those two were married for a whole six weeks. After the second Gabor, George went to Spain, drank heavily, and then killed himself.

Another blink-and-you'll-miss-it marriage was that of silent movie stars Jean Acker and Rudolph Valentino. They weren't exactly stars when they married, but it was just a matter of time for Rudy.

Just hours after they were married, Jean locked herself in the bathroom and wailed that she had made a terrible mistake. She later returned to the home of her former lover, actress Grace Diamond, and stayed with her. Not even the World's Greatest Lover could persuade Jean to return to him.

Carmen Electra and Dennis Rodman were married in November 1998. They divorced five months later. That was about four and half months longer than Rodman wanted to be Carmen's husband. He sought an annulment nine days after their Las Vegas nuptials, claiming that he didn't remember getting married because he was intoxicated at the time.

Actress Robin Givens and boxer Mike Tyson were married for a year, from February 1988 to February 1989, before she filed for divorce on grounds that he was physically abusive to her. A little older and wiser eight and a half years later, Robin married tennis instructor Syetozar Marinkovic on August 22, 1997, then dumped him on the very same day.

Then there's Bonny Lee Bakley, who was married ten times. While she was married to her second husband, who was also her cousin, she took a trip down South and introduced herself to the sister of rock 'n' roll legend Jerry Lee Lewis by doing a striptease in her living room, after which

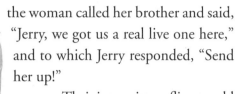

the woman called her brother and said, "Jerry, we got us a real live one here," and to which Jerry responded, "Send her up!"

Their intermittent fling would last nearly a decade and through several more of Bonny Lee's marriages—not to mention lovers and boyfriends that numbered in the hundreds, perhaps more. Bonny Lee's favorite hobby was bilking lonely men out of their money and having wild sex, with or without the cameras rolling.

Her shortest marriage was to Joseph Brooksher, her fifth husband; they were married for most of a day. Bonny stayed with her next husband, eighty-two-year-old William Weber of Florida, for about a week, just long enough to get her hands on $80,000 of his retirement money.

Bonny Lee's last husband was actor Robert Blake. They were married for six months, during which time, it is said, she also managed to squeeze in an affair with Christian Brando, Marlon Brando's son, and several dozen other hapless men who fell for her personal-ad scams.

Bonny Lee Bakley was murdered in a restaurant parking lot in 2001. Robert was the prime suspect, was imprisoned, and stood trial for the crime, but he was acquitted in 2005. There were, apparently, just too many people in the world besides Robert Blake who wanted her dead. Any one of them could have done it.

Going back a little further in history and before the current heyday of celebrity weddings is the legendary Pancho Villa. Pancho married most of the women who caught his eye as he went from town to town waging war and raising hell during the Mexican Revolution. In those days, proper young women of Spanish descent were brought up to hold on to their honor until their wedding night, so very few of them were going to give it up freely, not even for Pancho Villa.

So Pancho, crafty little soul that he was, bribed countless judges in every one of these towns to perform fake wedding ceremonies. In this manner, Pancho could consummate the marriage with the unsuspecting bride, then happily move on to his next conquest. No one knows for sure how many broken hearts and illegitimate children Pancho Villa left in his wake.

As of August 2007, the spry, one-legged sixty-year-old had seventy-eight children, ranging in age from three weeks to thirty-six years.

One man who knows exactly how many wives and children he's had—all of whom, by the way, are legitimate—is Daad Mohammed Murad Abdul Rahman from the United Arab Emirates. As of August 2007, the spry, one-legged sixty-year-old had seventy-eight children, ranging in age from three weeks to thirty-six years. He has had fifteen wives in all but had to divorce most of them along the way to comply with the law, which allows only four wives at a time. Fortunately, divorce is easy for Muslim men. They only have to say, "I divorce you!" three times, and it's done. They can submit the legal paperwork later.

Daad's work is not yet done, though. His plan is to have fathered one hundred children before his sixty-eighth birthday in the year 2015. After that, he will happily retire.

The holder of the Guinness world record for having the most legitimate marriages, however, goes to a man who is famous only because of the number of times he said, "I do." His name was Glynn Wolfe, and he was married a total of twenty-nine times before his death in 1998. His last wife, Linda Essex, was the runner-up for the Guinness record, having been married twenty-two times herself before she met Glynn.

Glynn died in Los Angeles at the age of eighty-eight. Despite leaving behind numerous still-living ex-wives, children, grandchildren, stepchildren, and countless ex-in-laws, no one claimed his body. Sadly, the city paid to have him buried in an unmarked grave.

There are many weirdly beloveds who were clearly driven by forces much more powerful than numbers.

Leo Tolstoy, for example, fell madly in love with a lovely young woman in 1862. She was a countess named Sophia Bers and was sixteen years younger than he. A week after he met her, he asked her to marry him.

This daughter of a prominent Moscow family knew that Tolstoy was not only a count, but also an author of world renown. What else on Earth did she need to know?

From his more mature point of view, Tolstoy knew there was plenty more to know. In fairness to her, and because he loved and trusted her, and because their courtship had been so short, he gave her dozens of his journals to read before the wedding.

The journals were filled with all manner of sordid details regarding Tolstoy's sexual exploits with a great many women, most of them poor serfs. Sophia started crying almost as soon as she began to read about them.

She was still crying when Tolstoy showed up just before the wedding to make sure she still wanted to marry him. She cried on the ride to the cathedral, and then really let loose during the ceremony. When the time came to say goodbye to her family and her hometown and follow her new husband to the unfamiliar and distant place where she would begin her life as Mrs. Leo Tolstoy, they practically had to pour her into the carriage to take her away.

There is an old wedding superstition that states that if a bride cries on her wedding day, they will be the last tears she sheds over her marriage. This was not the case for Sophia.

By most accounts, their forty-eight-year marriage was fueled by intense expressions of love and hate, as well as a great mutual respect for each other's opinions. Their relationship was also very often fraught with disagreements over a variety of fundamental philosophies and beliefs.

Toward the end, Sophia became convinced that Leo had changed his will behind her back. When he caught her ransacking his study in search of the document, Tolstoy became enraged. He boarded a train to get away from her. Again, Sophia cried.

Sadly, Tolstoy became very ill while onboard the train and died of pneumonia shortly thereafter.

Filled with remorse, Sophia spent the remainder of her own life crying over his loss.

A few years before the end of this tempestuously famous marriage, right around the time Leo and Sophia were celebrating their fortieth wedding anniversary, on the other side of the world a young Mexican couple were making plans to begin their own lives together as husband and wife.

Octavio Guillen asked his beloved, Adriana Martinez, for her hand in marriage. She happily said yes, but they decided to take things slowly.

They were married—finally—in 1969, after a sixty-seven-year engagement. They were both eighty-two on their wedding day.

It might have comforted Adriana to know that she was not the oldest known bride to be wheeled down the aisle. That honor goes to Minnie Munro from Point Clare, Australia. She was 102 years old in 1991 when she married Dudley Reid. Miss Minnie, that saucy little minx, practically robbed the cradle. Her Dudley was eighty-three when she happily took him as her husband.

The oldest known groom, however, was not Dudley Reid, but Harry Stevens of Wisconsin. He was 103 years old when he married the lovely Thelma, who was eighty-four at the time. The two celebrated their nuptials at the Caravilla Retirement Home in 1984.

Of all the people who marry more often than the norm, it's difficult to speculate over who might be happier, men or women. I find it interesting—and sad—that, despite his twenty-nine marriages, Glynn Wolfe's life ended in such a lonely way.

The opposite seems to have occurred with Many-Names, and my own great-aunt Angelina, a contemporary of Many-Names's who led a similarly colorful life.

These are, of course, too few data points from which to draw any serious conclusions, but it's interesting to study the comparisons between men like Glynn and women like Angelina and Many-Names.

Women of their generation were expected to fit into one of only a handful of roles—wife, mother, nurse, teacher, nun, maid, or librarian. Many-Names actually had been a lot of those things at one time or another. But she had also been the owner of a successful textile business, a state senator, and all-round pillar of her community in an era in which women were expected to blend into the wallpaper. My aunt Angelina managed to raise eleven nieces and nephews, the children of those of her siblings who had died young, leaving behind families that were still in need of maternal care. She finished raising all of those kids while blazing a trail for herself as a shrewd businesswoman who never let anyone get one over on her, a socially and politically involved member of her community, a trophy-winning ballroom dancer, and a real estate powerhouse. She marched in more parades and attended more parties than everyone else in our family combined.

Despite the fact that they never met and lived their lives in wildly different parts of the country, neither one of these amazing women feared stepping outside the narrow social mores of their times to become successful in their own right or shied away from love. Unlike Glynn, they died happy and wealthy old women in their seventies and eighties, with an astoundingly long trail of dead husbands and old boyfriends in their wake.

It wouldn't surprise me one bit to know they're both still racking up new conquests in the afterlife.

CHAPTER EIGHT

Byte Me

> *Naked* means you don't have
> any clothes on. *Nekkid* is when
> you don't have any clothes on,
> and you're up to no good.
>
> —LEWIS GRIZZARD

"We need to register a domain name for the company," our network manager announced ominously at a staff meeting one day. It was the early 1990s—the olden days, technologically speaking—and we were standing at the very precipice of the Internet Revolution.

We had no idea what that meant.

"Are you sure?" asked the department head, trying not to sound frightened.

"Yes," the network manager responded darkly.

Our boss put his hands on his hips, eyes darting rapidly from left to right. After a moment, he said, "Okay. Then what?"

"I don't . . . know," replied the network manager. "Nobody knows. We just know we need it. And we need it now, before it's too late."

"Too late for what?"

"I'm not sure."

So we got a dot-com name and set up a Web page that consisted mostly of our logo and a picture of the home office.

While businesses everywhere struggled to make sense of this terrible new beast, the horny people of the world had long figured out what it was for.

What penicillin and the pill did to ignite the sexual revolution of the 1960s was but a blip on the radar compared to the firestorm of eroticism that swept across the nation—and very soon afterward, the world—thanks to the sudden availability of affordable personal computers and a simple residential telephone connection. As we entered the last decade of the twentieth century, it was estimated that more than 80 percent of all Internet traffic was sex related.

People who, in their previous lives, had barely managed a nodding acquaintance with a QWERTY keyboard were now typing at the speed of light—and with one hand, no less! Heretofore respectable, churchgoing, law-abiding, regular, everyday folk began discovering their inner hairy nekkidness, and there was nothing that could stop them.

The sheer volume and variety of free virtual sex, accessible from the privacy of one's own home, was as mind-boggling as it was unprecedented. Best of all, people were discovering that they were not alone in their secret desires, curiosities, and derring-do. There were hundreds of thousands—perhaps millions—of other nekkid people gleefully seeking each other out, eager to welcome the newly nekkid into their virtual ranks, no longer relegated to fantasizing alone, in the dark, and in secret, finally able to wallow wantonly in the sheltering mists of anonymity.

They began naming their alter egos: BigDickWilly. DoubleDeeDee. Puddles.

There wasn't an honest soul among them.

In their online profiles, they described themselves as indefatigable stallions, insatiable vixens of lust, gods and goddesses of sexual prowess. They were beautiful beyond words, endowed to the gills. And now, finally, they had found a place where they could convince other people that they actually were all of these things. But it was even better than that. It was an entire community of people who needed to believe that there really was someplace in the universe where everyone—even them—had a fair chance of emerging victorious from the brutal and often dehumanizing competition for the perfect sexual conquest.

Yes, it was all make-believe and everybody knew it, but so what? Everyone was happy! Everybody was (sort of) getting laid! And you didn't even have to take a bath first! Nobody ever had a headache, nobody ever smelled of stale beer and three-day-old sweat, nobody ever had a period or skid marks in their shorts, and no one was ever asked to shave their legs or remove their ugly black ankle socks before getting into bed. Best of all, you couldn't get a disease, be killed by a jealous husband, or be forced to endure the laughter of a cruel woman. It was like we all died and went to Orgy Heaven.

So for most chat room divas and lotharios, a little fantasy role-playing was a perfectly harmless pastime. That it wasn't exactly real was only a minor detail. In the life of the mind, it was a thousand times more palpable and intense than reality itself and as addicting as heroin. "Besides," they said to their suspicious real-life spouses and lovers, "no one is getting hurt. It's no different from reading *Penthouse*. What's the big deal?"

That's what Adnan Klaric thought.

Adnan was a thirty-two-year-old Bosnian man from a town called Zenica. Tired of his harping wife's neglect and general all-round vitriol, he dubbed himself—of all things—"Prince of Joy" and logged on to an Internet chat room.

> *Adnan told "Sweetie" all about his miserable shrew of a wife. She typed sweet nothings at him and reassured him that he was wonderful, desirable, and undeserving of all that rancor.*

All Adnan wanted was a little gentle relief, an occasional reprieve from the acid bath his marriage had become. Before long, Adnan got his wish: A kind and gentle presence, aptly named "Sweetie," emerged from the ether to breathe new life into his poor battered soul.

Adnan told "Sweetie" all about his miserable shrew of a wife. She typed sweet nothings at him and reassured him that he was wonderful, desirable, and undeserving of all that rancor. She empathized point for point with every pang of his wretchedly aching heart. True love bloomed wildly amid the clicks and boops of their online relationship. They decided they had to meet.

When they showed up, they discovered that things were much more horrid than either one of them had imagined. For starters, they were *both* already married. The worst part? They were married to each other.

"Sweetie" turned out to be Adnan's real-life wife, Sara Klaric. Apparently, the "Piña Colada" song wasn't as big a hit in Bosnia.

The Klarics began divorce proceedings immediately, on the grounds of—what else?—online cheating.

Corporations eventually did figure out what to do with their dot-com sites, and the rest of us went shopping. Most Internet traffic these days is about buying stuff, reading about the stuff we want to buy, and bragging about the stuff we already bought. For years now, e-commerce has been giving e-sex a good run for its money. But, ingenious little things that we are, we have effectively figured out how to combine the two.

More than 80 per-
cent of men and
30 percent of women
now use their search engines to shop
online for love, sex, and romance . . . or some reasonable semblance of any of the above.

We also tend not to hide so coyly behind our imaginary sexual personae anymore. People still do use screen names and clever e-mail addresses to disguise their identities, at least to some extent, but we're no longer so terribly shy about revealing online who we are in real life. Perhaps this is due to the fact that, even more often than going online to look for sex, we now go there to look for real-life relationships. And for this, it's usually best to take a shower and show up as your real self.

Not that that happens all the time, either. Ask anyone who has attempted to match a perfectly coiffed and lip-glossed Glamour Shots photo, or a ten-year-old "seen better days and more hair" picture, to the face on the sad lump of humanity smiling hopefully—if a bit sheepishly—behind a tall mocha latte at the neighborhood coffee shop.

Even so, according to the research firm Marketing Vox, upwards of 28 percent of all adult Internet users spend more time online than they do in actual face-to-face contact with other human beings. Not surprisingly, almost as many admit that they're having little or no sex with in-the-flesh, live people.

It's difficult to estimate how many modern couples actually met online because, despite the rapidly disappearing stigma long attached to the "lonely hearts club" approach to dating, there's still enough discomfort in it for some people to feel compelled to keep that little secret to themselves. Most others simply don't bother notifying their online match-making services that they're now happily hitched. Still, with tens of millions of active members of online dating services, it's a rather safe bet that most couples who have hooked up in the last few years probably met online.

> *Still, with tens of millions of active members of online dating services, it's a rather safe bet that most couples who have hooked up in the last few years probably met online.*

It is, of course, a far cry from the way most of our grand-parents and all of their forebears met and married. They tended to live their whole lives in the same town and knew all the same people. For the most part, they met each other in school or church, or were introduced by well-intentioned friends and family.

Before the 1950s, most marriages were often little more than good business arrangements. Farmers married strong, sturdy women to help with the backbreaking work; rich men married pretty little things, or not-so-pretty ones with lots of old money and very generous dowries. Whatever the circumstances of their initial meeting, they tended to stay married to the bitter end.

Still, it feels like a bit of a cop-out to assume that people like our great-grandparents, who met "the normal way," had marriages that lasted longer than they do nowadays because they didn't do that crazy Internet thing or try dating a thousand people before finally picking one. I have another theory, and it has nothing to do with the meeting. It has everything to do with the dumping.

If Grandma had been able to speed-type an e-mail message to Grandpa and hit the SEND button before she could regain her ladylike composure, she surely would never have endured his bed farts for fifty-seven years. She would have ended it swiftly, while she was still young and beautiful and free, perhaps by firing off a little missive like this:

Sherman, you putz,

I saw you looking up that tramp Mary Louise's skirt today as she shimmied up the fire escape like an alley cat in heat on her way up to the roof. I KNEW something was going on when, all of a sudden, you needed to check on the pigeon coop. WHAT PIGEONS?! Since when do you keep pigeons on the roof of MY building??? This just proves one thing, Sherman. You're an even bigger putz than people have been telling me.

Fare thee well, Sherman, and may you die a thousand horrible deaths. You putz.

Yours never more,
Irma

P.S. Notice your ma's e-mail address on the CC line of this message. And those of my gigantic, bloodthirsty brothers, those animals. And everyone else in my address book. And just wait until my 853 MySpace friends see this. You putz.

Without e-mail and its powerful ability to let Irma spew instantly and without interruption the venom that was consuming her in the blistering heat of that bitter moment of betrayal, she would have had to confront Sherman the Putz some other way. Sitting down to write him a regular letter would have required her to get some stationery, find a pen, write very slowly (compared to the rapid-fire pounding her computer keyboard would have taken), fold the paper, put it in an envelope, address the envelope, buy a stamp, walk to the mailbox, wait three to six days for a response or reaction . . . way too much time to cool down and reconsider things. The alternative, which would have been confronting Sherman face-to-face, would have given him the opportunity to explain himself, beg for forgiveness, deny the obvious, and/or convince Irma that she was hallucinating.

The expediency and lightning speed of e-mail guarantees that, once it's out there, you can't take it back. And because an electronic confrontation isn't as devastating a personal attack as, say, a head-on automobile collision, it would also have been a lot easier for Sherman to walk away from the whole mess without responding at all.

Either way, this is probably why the Irmas and the Shermans of yore ended up getting married anyway, and then stayed together for decades on end until one of them dropped dead, just like they promised.

Of course, Irma and Sherman are hypothetical people I made up to illustrate a point—not that there aren't hundreds of thousands of real-life examples of the Electronic Dump zipping madly through the cyber universe at any given time.

One of my favorites was written by a woman from Washington State, who, in November 2006, wrote a five-page diatribe to Jennifer, the purported "dumb drunk bitch from the tweaker's house" who stole her husband. "Pissed Off Wife," as she called herself, posted the letter in a public forum on the wildly popular Internet site Craigslist, where it has been read, forwarded, and reposted elsewhere on the Web by countless millions of readers and is still being read all these years later.

Pissed Off Wife went to great lengths to spell out for Jennifer all that she had "won" in the bargain, not the least of which was the ex-husband's unfortunate back injury, which she could forevermore blame for his inability to achieve a worthwhile erection.

She also made it clear that she was going to make it her mission in life to consume every spare moment of her ex's life with petty errands and demands—on behalf of the children, of course. On the bright side, Jennifer would inherit a few fun tasks, such as replenishing the

> *Pissed Off Wife did her best to end the letter with a touch of grace: "He's all yours you fucking whore!"*

ex's wardrobe. "You see, after he stepped from [the] shower this morning," Pissed Off Wife explained, "a giant black hole appeared in my home and devoured almost all of his clothing. Therefore, he will come to you almost naked (lucky you). The bright side is that you can dress him any way you want. Go nuts and buy him a leash and some vinyl attire, or a cute little dress while you're at it!"

Pissed Off Wife did her best to end the letter with a touch of grace: "He's all yours you fucking whore!"

That had to feel good . . . even if it was only for a few minutes.

One of the most memorable e-dumps of all time, however, has to be the fifteen-page rant that Dr. Nicholas Bartha of New York City sent in July 2006. The electronic message was addressed to his soon-to-be ex-wife, Fox News, Arnold Schwarzenegger, some of Dr.  Bartha's colleagues and neighbors, Senator Chuck Schumer, several other politicians, a few international news outlets, and just about everyone in his address book.

Among other things that had nothing to do with his marriage, Dr. Bartha told his wife that he would never surrender half of his net worth to her in their impending divorce—especially not the estimated $2 million Mrs. Bartha was expecting as part of the property settlement with regard to their beautiful Upper East Side townhouse.

"When you read this," Bartha told his wife and everyone else on the distribution list, "your life will change forever . . . You will be transformed from gold digger . . . to rubbish digger."

Shortly after hitting the SEND button, he blew himself up and took the building with him.

As luck would have it, the empty lot where the townhouse once stood was sold at auction for $8 million. The former Mrs. Bartha got her settlement after all, and Dr. Bartha's e-mail will live forever on the Internet.

Before they installed on-ramps on the information super-highway, the so-called mail-order bride business had been popular for centuries. By most accounts, the idea took off when lonely colonists and settlers wrote plaintive letters back home bemoaning the lack of eligible young women in the New World. Enterprising matchmakers from England to Hong Kong immediately went to work assembling their catalogs, "picture bride" introductory letters, and their price lists.

Very few men and women who have actually wed through such commercial means are likely to admit to it publicly. But here comes the Internet, once again, to the rescue! No longer having to hide the daily mail from the prying eyes of a nosy landlady or an overbearingly possessive mother, the would-be groom can finally shop for a woman the way God intended: in private and by the glow of a computer screen.

It was, not surprisingly, a rather small leap between the mail-order-bride business and the somewhat less egregious notion of Internet dating. Certain sites make no bones about existing for the sole purpose of getting marriage-minded people together. Countless other sites are equally candid about their missions to facilitate sexual encounters, or to serve people caught in the terrible cycle of obsessive-compulsive serial dating. And there's a personal introduction site for every possible predilection and sexual permutation imaginable. Here are just a few:

HornyMatches.com *(self-explanatory)*

FarmersOnly.com *(for farmers, ranchers, cowboys, cowgirls, and other country folk)*

LonelyWivesAffairs.com *(home of the Cheating Wives Club)*

SugarDaddie.com *(millionaire dating, as seen on Dr. Phil)*

NaughtyorNice.com *(covering all the bases)*

OnlineBootyCall.com *(slogan: "Don't Promise Marriage— Just Date!")*

CrazyKinky.com *(self-explanatory . . . I think)*

Marry-An-Ugly-Millionaire-Online-Dating-Agency.com *(gay or straight)*

BOOMj.com *(for the senior set, or those fast approaching "a certain age")*

DateMyPet.com *(for pet lovers in search of each other, not for their pets)*

PolyamoryConnection.com *(for those seeking multiple simultaneous bed-buddies)*

VeganPassions.com *(for those who will eat nothing with a face, no pun intended)*

TheSpankingNews.com *(for naughty fans of rosy bottoms)*

CelibatePassions.com *(for those who want no sex at all)*

Although it would seem that there could be no possible reason in the world for anyone from any walk of life *not* to find a partner online, amazingly, the mail-order-bride business continues to thrive.

A study conducted by the Global Survival Network in the late 1990s estimated that more than two hundred companies were providing wife-finding services to as many as five thousand American men a year. This created a terrible mental image for me—that of a lonely middle-aged man thumbing through the pages of a mail-order-bride catalog with one elbow propped on the toilet-paper roll and his shorts puddled around his ankles. For this reason alone I'm rather glad the paper version of the catalog business is practically extinct, thanks to the Internet.

"Find-a-wife" Web sites have sprouted up everywhere, slowly replacing the old-fashioned paper catalog. There's one called NatashaClub.com, which offers "Sexy Ukrainian Brides!" among its more than twenty-five thousand Russian women up for grabs (so to speak).

I believe there are several reasons why the international marital hookup as a business endures despite the incredible glut of free and pay-through-the-nose Internet dating sites: First, there will always be men who are convinced that foreign women are more beautiful, docile, and/or subservient than their brassy, outspoken, and independent American counterparts. Secondly, there are a lot of men who prefer women who can't speak English; with a wife like that, a man will never have to explain himself to her or pretend to listen to endlessly pointless female chatter. Lastly, there must be some proportion of these men who simply lack the skills or the self-confidence to get through a first date with any woman, even a desperate one with a screaming "Come Get Me!" ad on an online dating site.

Considering the high cost of sending away for a wife from a catalog or Web site ($10 or more for each letter to correspond with a prospective bride, plus the agency's finder's fee, the cost of obtaining a passport and visa for the girl, and another couple of thousand dollars for shipping and handling), clearly the overwhelming majority of these men are not in bad financial shape. It's not that they can't afford to buy a local woman a cup of coffee or a nice meal on a first date. I mean, they couldn't be *that* cheap . . . could they? Let's assume not. Let's just say they're socially inept.

> *Considering the high cost of sending away for a wife from a catalog or Web site, clearly the overwhelming majority of these men are not in bad financial shape.*

If you're thinking I sound an awful lot like I'm picking on poor lonely men, let us take note, please, that the mail-order-*husband* catalog never took off in quite the same way. I don't think that's an accident.

There have been a few reasonable enough substitutes, though. Magazines consisting almost entirely of personal ads for men and women were extremely prolific in virtually every major city in the nation during the 1980s. Personal ads in local newspapers are still very common.

One of the most ingenious low-tech methods of publishing personal ads came about fairly recently. A handful of farmers from Wales got the bright idea to advertise themselves on the backs of milk cartons.

One of them, thirty-year-old Iwan Jones, from a tiny place in the Welsh countryside called Groes, pointed out that his neck of the woods "is a hard place to find a date," and that about a quarter of all farmers are single men. They tried to form a support group, but it felt a little weird. So they went with the milk carton thing, effectively combining business and pleasure. So far, it's working rather well.

Still, this isn't quite the same as a mail-order-husband catalog. I do believe the reason that exact approach never quite sprouted wings has to do with opportunity meeting some reasonable semblance of female propriety, together with a man's own willingness to advertise himself, and women finally deciding they would no longer be coy about making the first move.

I have no doubt there are women out there looking for nonworkaholic swarthy lovers with sexy foreign accents who have no interest in baseball and can dance a mean tango. Men like that tend to be a little harder to find in places like Booger Holler, Arkansas. A catalog or reasonable substitute would come in rather handy.

Women can and do, in effect, go shopping for husbands and lovers on any one of several hundred Internet dating sites, and the most it will cost them is the price of a monthly subscription. And if such a woman is aware that she'll probably get what she pays for, there are many more free and bargain-basement sites from which to choose.

WEIRDLY BELOVED

According to a 2003 article in the *U.S. News and World Report,* it was estimated that upwards of forty million individuals in the United States visit online dating sites in a single month. That was about half the number of all American singles at the time.

A more recent report by the marketing organization Jupiter Research stated that, in 2007, German men and women spent more than 85 million euros (about $126 million American dollars) looking for love online. They projected that figure to exceed 103 million euros by the end of 2008.

It would appear that the stigma of online dating is beginning to fade a little.

These astoundingly high enrollment numbers and dollar amounts also demonstrate that women are not only willing participants in the proactive search for lovers, partners, and spouses, but that they have the financial and logistical means—not to mention the mental and emotional fortitude—to do so. They have, in effect, turned the concept of "mail-order bride" completely on its head and proven unequivocally that what's good for the gander is good for the goose.

Match.com, arguably the most popular dating site in the world, boasts more than fifteen million members from no fewer than 246 countries. Approximately 40 percent of the currently active members are women. Not all of them are looking for husbands, though. On this site, you can be a woman looking for a woman, a man looking for a man, or any old sort of free spirit just looking for a warm place to put it. You don't even have to be single. All you have to be is willing to lie about your marital status.

eHarmony, on the other hand, specifically targets a traditional (read "one man, one woman") marriage-minded audience. They're also considering implementing some kind of identity verification protocol into their system to better weed out the creeps and provide its members with some semblance of security.

eHarmony currently claims more than three million members. Unlike Match.com, you do have to be heterosexual, over the age of twenty-one, legally single, and well employed enough to be able to plop down about fifty of your hard-earned bucks a month until you find your perfect match, or until you can no longer stand the mercilessly byzantine structure of the site's profile setup and mate-selection process.

eHarmony members are mostly white, well-educated professionals, and predominantly Christian. They are also overwhelmingly female. Women in their thirties make up about 70 percent of the membership.

So there's your respectable, modern-day, multimillion-dollar mail-order-husband business. It's the brainchild of Dr. Neil Clark Warren, a self-described conservative Christian psychologist and frequent advertiser on Rush Limbaugh's pathologically antiliberal radio program.

Oh, look . . . a report just handed to me states that Mr. Limbaugh is currently an active member of eHarmony.

He's all yours, girls.

Chapter Nine

Catered Affairs to Remember

> MY FIANCÉ AND I are having a little disagreement. What I want is a big church wedding with bridesmaids and flowers and a no-expense-spared reception; what he wants is to BREAK OFF OUR ENGAGEMENT.
>
> —SALLY POPLIN
> (BRITISH COMEDIENNE)

A couple of months before my wedding, I was summoned for jury duty. Forty or fifty of my fellow citizens and I sat in a courtroom, along with a handful of lawyers and the two young men who were about to stand trial for murder. The younger and smaller of the defendants, little more than a baby, looked terrified. The other bigger one was just plain terrifying.

Little by little, lawyers from both sides worked to whittle down the assemblage to an even dozen, plus however many alternate jurors they select for these things. I never did find out how many they ended up choosing. I was whittled out pretty early on.

The lawyers asked questions like, "Has anyone close to you ever been murdered?" and "Is there any reason why you feel you might not be emotionally capable of participating in this trial?"

It was that "emotionally capable" question that did me in.

There were a million reasons why I would have found it difficult to stand in judgment of those two young men, and a million other reasons why I would have loved to participate in that trial. But I raised my hand, as I knew I should, and responded as honestly as I could. When I opened my mouth to speak, what came out was the voice of a lunatic.

"Well," I began, and then all the maniacs in my head got loose: "I'm about to be married, see? And I still haven't finalized the menu with the caterer, and I think the lady who's making my dress is never going to finish it because she just took a job with Kimberly-Clark and she's never in her shop anymore! And my fiancé and I, we bought this house to get married in—and also to live in later, of course—well, we're living in it now, but I don't know how—*it's the stupidest house I've ever seen!!!*—I don't know how in the world am I going to get thirty or forty chairs into that teeny-tiny living room that looked so huge when the realtor showed it to us—and I know, I know, I know, I know, this isn't relevant to the question, I'm sorry, and it probably doesn't matter anyway because *nobody's* coming to this dumb wedding, I just know it, so I probably should just go ahead and do my jury duty. But the invitations are already out, and I still have a *billion things*—"

"Thank you, ma'am," one of the lawyers said. "and . . . uh . . . good luck with all that."

Then they sent me home.

And that poor little skinny terrified kid sank even lower into his chair. I wanted to hit myself in the head with a hammer.

A wedding can turn anyone into a blithering idiot, or, in the worst of cases, a full-blown psycho. I don't care how smart or how sane you were before the engagement; we're all suscepti-ble. And if you tend to live your normal life dangling by your fingertips from the crumbling ledges of reality, as I occasion-ally do, it's a sure bet things are going to get a little weird.

I'm proud to say that the jury duty episode was my most demented premarital moment. There were others, I'm sure, but that was the worst.

The wedding itself was quite lovely, though. A small gathering of good friends in our not-really-stupid-after-all home, delicious food, beautiful flowers, a pretty little cake . . . very simple. We blew most of the wedding budget on a shamelessly self-indulgent honeymoon in Paris and had the time of our lives. If I had to do it all over again, I'd do it exactly the same way, but without the jury duty and with a different husband.

While this approach turned out to be perfect for us, I do understand that it simply won't do for most married couples. It's all about the dress and the party, and the ultimate realization of lifelong dreams and Hollywood-inspired fantasies coming, at long last, to life.

The prize for "unique and simple"—if there were such a prize—would almost certainly go to British comedian Paul Merton and his beloved, Sarah Parkinson, a writer and producer in the entertainment business. They went to a desert island in the middle of the Indian Ocean to get married. There were no guests present; no priests, ministers, or justices of the peace; no witnesses of any kind. In fact, except for Paul and Sarah on that day in May 2000, the tiny speck of land was completely uninhabited. The couple was dropped off by the captain of a small boat, handed a picnic basket and a walkie-talkie, and left alone to wed in private. They read their vows to each other and pronounced themselves husband and wife.

I can't imagine how any other wedding could beat that one for being both bare-bones and extraordinary all at the same time.

At the other extreme, the 1916 wedding of Kamala Kaul and Jawaharlal Nehru, India's first prime minister, is a serious contender for most elaborate. The celebration, which took place in the city of Delhi, lasted more than a month and a half. Guests were entertained with badminton and tennis marathons, countless dinner parties, musical performances, and traditional poetry readings. Afterward, all of the men in the wedding party headed for the hills—literally. They spent the next month in the mountains of the Zojila Pass on a hunting trip.

During my own wedding reception, my new husband disappeared for about twenty minutes to take a spin in his friend's beautiful new BMW convertible. I wanted to kill them both for that.

Tropical paradise weddings are, of course, the stuff of dreams—at least for those who've never lived on an island. I can tell you from personal experience that a hundred yards of silk, taffeta, and tulle in ninety-degree heat makes for one smelly bridal party. These things have to be carefully thought out.

If I were one of those phony psychics, I would be on the lookout for anyone named Pamela and/or Lee. Then I would tell him, her, or them that I see tropical islands and unconventionally clad friends in their marital futures. The next few stories will illustrate why.

Scottish comedian Billy Connolly and his wife, Pamela Stephenson, had the right idea when they chose to celebrate their wedding in Fiji in 1989. They printed their wedding invitations on the sarongs they wanted their guests to wear for the occasion.

Billy and Pamela weren't exactly on the island when the magical moment happened; more accurately, they were in the water, about waist-deep. Also very smart, considering the climate.

The bride was given away by the wonderfully outrageous Dame Edna Everage, who, when not in full drag, is a man named Barry Humphries.

I would have loved to have been a guest at that wedding.

In August 2007, a couple in their fifties identified only as Pam and Lee walked down the aisle in the Berkshire Mountains on a gorgeous late-summer morning. Except for a few hats and shawls, the overwhelming majority of their six hundred guests gathered on the beautiful green hilltop completely in the nude.

Only a dozen or so spoilsports were fully clothed. Even the bride and groom figurines that topped the cake were naked. Lee, the groom, was more elaborately dressed than his bride, Pam; he was decked out in a bow tie and top hat.

Pam and Lee are part of an ever-growing movement to bring the nudist lifestyle into the mainstream. They are working very hard to breathe new life into stale old traditions, most especially those related to wedding celebrations.

Nudity is not about sex, they say, as many fully clothed people believe. It's about a sense of spirituality and acceptance missing from too many of our lives. "God keeps sending us naked people," Lee says, "and we keep sending him people that are all dressed."

Naked weddings certainly have their perks. You can put one together practically for free, especially if you do it outside and on a warm day, and you bake the cake yourself.

In 1995, actress Pamela Anderson chose as her wedding attire a white bikini when she married musician Tommy Lee the first time. The two had known each other for a whole ninety-six hours before they decided to tie the knot.

The ceremony, which was held on a beach in Cancún, Mexico, took place with Pam and Tommy stretched out on lounge chairs and sipping cocktails. They later had a more formal wedding ceremony. For that one they wore silver space suits.

Eschewing the paradise theme altogether, a couple from Simi Valley in California arranged to have their wedding take place much closer to home. They hired the Reverend Robert E. Cote to perform the ceremony on Halloween night.

Reverend Robert, as he likes to be called, describes himself as "the only wedding officiant doing twenty-first-century,

Theta-Level wedding ceremonies" (by which he means that he works from "inside of God").

He's not a minister in the traditionally ordained sense. He doesn't exactly have a congregation, either, or a building anyone might think of as a church. His temple is the Earth itself.

Still, he has performed countless weddings designed especially for couples with that special taste for the unconventional. Perhaps most notable among them is (presumably) the first gay wedding on board the *Queen Mary* off the coast of California. This was one of Reverend Robert's trademark "clandestine wedding settings"—places with special meaning to the couple but that are not necessarily contracted in the usual way. "It's easier to ask forgiveness than permission," the reverend says. The wedding took place without a hitch, but they were all asked to leave as soon as it was over.

The Simi Valley couple's Halloween ceremony was not at all clandestine. It took place on the steps of a haunted house called the Screams and was broadcast live on KISS-FM radio. A professional makeup artist from Hollywood made Reverend Robert up to look like a dead monk.

The bride's Catholic mother was, of course, appropriately horrified by all this, but Reverend Robert smoothed things over by pointing out during the ceremony that this wedding was, in fact, taking place on the eve of All Saints' Day, one of the Church's favorite holy days. He also reminded everyone that Halloween itself was properly absconded from the pagans centuries ago, so God was undoubtedly happy to bless this union in such a joyously creative way.

There was no word indicating whether the mother didn't burst a few blood vessels anyway.

Tina Milhoane and Robert Seifer had a similar idea when they tied the knot in October 2007. The couple, both in their twenties, had worked at a Halloween attraction called 7 Floors of Hell in Berea, Ohio, for the past four years. It was only natural they would consider this their home away from home.

Six pallbearers brought Robert in a coffin to the cemetery of the haunted house. Guests were dressed lavishly as witches, ghouls, and an assortment of undead characters.

Robert's father said the experience was a little weird but acknowledged that stranger things have happened. At least his son wasn't getting married in a skydiving ceremony.

There's a red-roof wedding chapel in Hell. About thirty couples got married there last February 29th.

It was an actual cold day in Hell, a tiny hamlet in rural Michigan. Snow fell earlier in the day, delaying the arrival of a few of the couples.

The event was organized by John Colone, the unofficial mayor of Hell. Colone is also the proprietor of the Screams Ice

Cream and Halloween Store, behind which the little red chapel is located.

A nondenominational minister named Ann Jarema performed the weddings for free in honor of leap year in 2008. The chapel was booked solid from 8:30 in the morning until 9:30 that night. Hairdressers and photographers were also on hand to assist with last-minute requests for services. After their respective ceremonies, many of the couples went next door to the Dam Site Inn for a special wedding dinner.

Brides and grooms showed up from far and wide, many of them decked out in leather, red and black, and other non-traditional attire. Well-wishers lined the roadside leading to Hell's chapel holding up signs printed with such sentiments as TURN BACK and the international symbol for death, the skull and crossbones.

Theodore Raios, one of the grooms, was formerly a forty-two-year-old bachelor who had sworn Hell would freeze over before he ever got married. So when it did, he did. And as fate would have it, he married a young woman named Angel.

In June 2007 in South Korea, Seok Gyeong-jae and his bride, Daejeon, arranged for a rather unusual master of ceremonies to assist at their wedding. Tiro, a robot created by Seok, performed admirably. In a man's voice, Tiro introduced the couple to the guests and carried out all of his preprogrammed emcee duties throughout the reception. Other androids were also in attendance, serving as ushers and entertainers.

All of the mechanical men were very well behaved, especially considering that South Korean robots are usually deployed as guards in schools and as machine-gun-toting sentinels along the heavily fortified North Korean border. Thankfully, there were no reports of casualties at Seok Gyeong-jae and Daejeon's wedding . . . nor of any unruly guests.

Nothing was going to keep Kaylee Gleeson from marching down that aisle and marrying her beloved, Josh Kelly. In February 2008, held together with a bunch of wires, metal rods, and other assorted hardware, she did just that.

Six months before, Kaylee had broken her back in three places when she flipped her motorcycle in a friendly race against her fiancé and some friends. Doctors weren't sure she'd ever walk again, but thanks to modern medical technology and the determination of this fearless daredevil bride, Kaylee got to dance at her own wedding.

Sometimes the bride and groom manage to remain reasonably sane throughout the whole crazy-making wedding-planning process, and even all the way through the end of the festivities. It's their relatives who lose their minds.

In 1918, fourteen-year-old Princess Nagako was chosen by the Imperial Household Ministry of Japan to wed Prince Hirohito. When it was discovered that the princess was color-blind, court officials demanded that Prince Kuni, Nagako's father, rescind his daughter's betrothal. Kuni refused to bring such dishonor upon his family. So he offered to stab his daughter to death and then kill himself.

A horrified public, and an even more horrified Emperor Taisho, decided that it might not be so bad after all to let the wedding take place as planned. They would take their chances and hope that the heirs would not inherit their mother's less-than-perfect eyesight. The couple got married, and no one had to be stabbed.

In one of history's worst cases of meddling old aunts, the empress dowager of China, Tzu-hsi, took it upon herself to arrange the nuptials of her nephew, Kuang-hsu, in 1889. His was not the first marriage she would orchestrate in order to keep the power on her side of the family and, more specifically, in her hands. She ordered that Kuang-hsu marry his cousin Yehonala, a girl he loathed, and who hated him just as intensely despite her shy and submissive demeanor.

Determined to stop the wedding, Kuang-hsu set fire to the wedding canopies. The ceremony took place anyway.

In the end, all of Auntie Tzu-hsi's plans were for naught. Since Kuang-hsu refused to have anything to do with his bride and preferred instead to take his concubine into his bed, producing an heir with Yehonala was a logistical conundrum. Tzu-hsi never got her pedigreed heir.

Kuang-hsu eventually rebelled against Tzu-hsi and, as emperor, issued many decrees in an attempt to modernize China's political and social structure, and probably also just to piss off his aunt. The empress took back the throne in 1898 and had Kuang-hsu imprisoned for the rest of his life.

On her deathbed, Tzu-hsi arranged the marriage of another nephew, an infant named Pu-yi. Two months before his third birthday, that child would become the last emperor of China, and later the subject of Bernardo Bertolucci's 1987 Academy Award–winning film.

A few centuries earlier and on another continent, Jofré Borgia married the sweet sixteen-year-old maiden Sancha of Aragon in 1494. The entire wedding party accompanied the newly-weds into the marital bedchamber, and then stayed there to watch—not because they were kinky, but because, well . . . they were in Europe, and this is how the rich and powerful did things in that part of the world in those days. Also, Jofré was only about twelve years old at the time and might have needed a little guidance.

The bridesmaids undressed the couple and placed them on the marital bed. Then the king, the papal emissaries, and members of the consul arrived. While the entire entourage looked on and commented amongst themselves, the young couple consummated their marriage.

Five or six years later, His Holiness Pope Alexander VI ordered his son (yes, his son), Cesare Borgia, to renounce his role as cardinal, give up his clerical vows, and find a suitable wife in order to keep political power within the family. Cesare was also Jofré's older brother; His Holiness had many children, and more than a few lovers, along the way.

Like his father, Cesare was a bit of a wild man. He hired an herbalist to concoct an aphrodisiac for him and his bride, Charlotte d'Albret. The happy couple drank their fill of the brew on their wedding night, only to discover shortly thereafter that the beverage they drank was actually an extremely potent laxative.

Cesare and Charlotte survived their wedding night, albeit a bit more dehydrated than they originally planned.

Proving once again that the apple rarely falls far from the tree, Cesare went on to take many lovers throughout his married life, including his sister-in-law, Sancha of Aragon.

Arranged marriages and weddings in which the family has the ultimate say are by no means relics of the past. In November 2007, an entire village got into the act when a groom from Bihar's Arwal district in India showed up to his own wedding in a drunken stupor. Outraged, the family decreed that the bride should marry her fiancé's brother, who, lucky for him, happened to be stone cold sober at the moment. The brother was all too happy to marry the pretty teenage girl. The villagers then chased the drunk ex-fiancé all the way out of town.

Madho Singh, a senior police officer in the district, reported that the groom eventually sobered up and returned to the village. He has been spotted on several occasions crying over the loss of his bride and worrying that no one will ever want to marry him now. The villagers remain unmoved.

Another outraged father made history—or at least the six o'clock news—in June 2007 when he found out that his daughter had moved in with her fiancé. Mohd Nasher of Middletown Township in Pennsylvania was so outraged by the dishonor this brought upon the entire family that he enlisted the help of his son, Mohammed. Together they went to make things right for all involved.

When they arrived at the young man's house, Mohd and Mohammed dragged him into the family's SUV, beat him up, and told him they were going to take him to "an undisclosed location."

It was this last suggestion that made the would-be son-in-law's survival instincts kick into high gear. He broke free from Mohd and Mohammed and managed to escape from the SUV. As soon as he was able, he called the police.

The Nasher men explained to the cops that this was all an unfortunate misunderstanding based on cultural differences. Surely the officers could see how Mohd had no choice but to beat the crap out of the fiancé in defense of the family's honor. Mohd and Mohammed were arrested and booked on assault and kidnapping charges.

The young couple fled Pennsylvania and were, at last reports, living a normal life, still together. A family spokeswoman, threatening to sue if the story was made public, told a local NBC News reporter, "That's the problem with this country! We put everything on TV!" It would seem she was somewhat less disturbed by the concept of beating up and kidnapping another human being. She also appeared not to be terribly opposed to grand old American traditions, like yelling, "Lawsuit!" at the first sign of insult.

Another case of family and friends getting a little carried away at a wedding happened at a catering hall called GiGi's in Flint, Michigan, in 2003. The couple, whose names were obscured in the police report, had invited thirty-one-year-old construction worker and convicted felon Michael VanStrate to their wedding. VanStrate, a bear of a man at six feet, two inches tall and 260 pounds, had had a bit too much to drink that night and started picking fights with the other guests, including a nine-year-old boy. When the boy's father intervened, VanStrate bit off the man's right index finger. VanStrate then attempted to do the same to the groom's thumb. When the groom's mother got in the way, VanStrate knocked her out with an elbow to the head.

It took several local law enforcement officers and state troopers to subdue VanStrate. He was arraigned on two counts of assault with "intent to do great bodily harm less than murder," one count of aggravated assault, and one count of simple assault.

Just one week later, another wedding brawl broke out in Michigan at the Ogemaw County Fairgrounds, where the Evers family was celebrating their daughter's wedding to Tom Harrison. The bride's brothers—Scott, Erik, Aaron, Ryan, and Randall—became a bit distraught when the bar closed as the reception came to an end.

Scott, who had just lost an arm-wrestling match with his new brother-in-law, was the first to notice that the bar was closing. So he sucker-punched the bartender, Jon Krupa, and went home. Brother Aaron took over, biting Krupa on the nose. When Krupa fell to the ground, Randall kicked him in the head.

Pamela Straub, a brave disc jockey hired to entertain the guests, stepped in when she saw what was happening to the poor bartender. That's when Randall stopped kicking Krupa, called Pamela a whore, pushed her against a wall, and knocked her unconscious.

Jason Oliver, a friend of Pamela the DJ, was then punched by Randall, apparently for having not had sense enough to look away while he was attacking Pamela. Jason lost a few teeth in the incident.

When the police arrived, Scott, of course, had already left the scene. However, they were able to take the remaining brothers into custody. During the arrest, Aaron pushed a deputy in the chest, head-butted one of the troopers in the nose, and caused significant damage to the patrol car. Randall was arrested for assaulting the bartender, the DJ, and the DJ's friend. Ryan and Erik were both charged with assaulting each other.

Now *there's* a wedding story for the grandkids.

Two unrelated wedding receptions that took place at the Granite Rose, a popular banquet hall in New Hampshire, became one giant blood-and-puke fest on an otherwise lovely September evening in 2007.

The Granite Rose had two ballrooms available for wedding receptions and other large parties. The restrooms were considered a common area to be shared by all guests at the facility. The problems seemed to stem from the fact that the two brides and their respective guests turned out to be of wildly different temperaments, unequal alcohol tolerances, and disparate notions regarding proper etiquette in a public space.

In her lawsuit against the Granite Rose, Marcy Milbury claims that management did nothing when her bridesmaids were attacked by the other bride and some of her female guests in the ladies' room. According to Marcy, all the women from the other party were drunk, including the bride, and that they then proceeded to throw up all over the place. Also, she said, the other bride's increasingly inebriated guests kept using Marcy's banquet room as a shortcut to the lavatories.

Shortly after midnight, management finally threw both parties out of the building, but by then the hostilities between the two groups had escalated to the point at which the only possible resolution seemed to be an old-fashioned fistfight in the parking lot. Nearly one hundred guests from both sides were involved in the melee.

Marcy hopes to recover the $18,175 she paid for the reception and collect unspecified damages for the immeasurable emotional distress she suffered on her painstakingly planned wedding day. The other bride claims her recollection of the events was a little different from Marcy's. The case is still pending.

"Marry a nice dentist," my Aunt Vivian would say.[8] "They make excellent providers."

That may be so, but sometimes they're just like normal people.

Christa from Pennsylvania married a nice dentist, Dr. David Wielechowski. They got into an awful row only hours after promising to love, honor, et cetera in the spring of 2008.

Two people heard Christa screaming on the seventh floor of the Holiday Inn where they had just held their wedding reception. They found the couple fully engaged in a fistfight. The guests attempted to rescue the bride from the angry groom, only to have the newlyweds turn their rage on them. The police report stated that Christa and her new hubby began hurling metal planters at the would-be rescuers, causing them injuries that included broken bones, knocked-out teeth, and several skin lacerations.

The bride and her nice dentist were hauled off to jail, David still wearing most of his tuxedo and with one black eye swollen shut. Christa was tossed into her very own prison cell, wedding dress and all.

---

[8] Aunt Viv is my inner Jewish mother. She lives in one of the attic rooms inside my head.

Then there's the sad tale of a bride who, understandably, prefers to remain anonymous. During her engagement, she worked overtime to pay for the wedding of her dreams. Unlike her, her fiancé was from a wealthy family. They were of the very strong opinion that it was strictly the responsibility of the bride's parents to foot the bill. When the bride-to-be suggested postponing the wedding to give herself more time to save up enough money to pay for everything herself, the love of her life threatened never to speak to her again. She decided to marry him anyway, and on the date they had originally set.

At the church a year and a half later, when her mother realized the ceremony was being officiated by a nonde-nominational minister, she

> *To Dr. Klein's credit, she pointed out that a wedding and a marriage were two different things. The "do-over" wasn't going to fix her mother, or make the insensitive lout she had married a better husband.*

began screaming that her daughter had joined a cult, and then proceeded to faint. Things went downhill from there.

Three years later, the not-so-new bride found herself seeking advice from psychologist and columnist Dr. Louise Klein, asking if she should divorce her husband and have a "do-over" now that she was better employed and able to pay for the beautiful and lavish celebration she had always envisioned for herself—preferably without her mother in attendance, but apparently, with the same gem of a guy she had originally chosen.

To Dr. Klein's credit, she pointed out that a wedding and a marriage were two different things. The "do-over" wasn't going to fix her mother, or make the insensitive lout she had married a better husband.

Of course, Dr. Klein was much more diplomatic in her response than that, but that was pretty much the gist of it.

Not all weddings in which the family becomes overly involved need end in tragedy or incarceration.

There's a British television sitcom called *The Vicar of Dibley* about the day-to-day antics of a rather unconventional clergywoman. Fans of the show might find it rather amusing that a real life Vicar of Dibley lives and walks among us.

The Reverend Marian Sturrock made history in England in August 2000 when she became the first female priest to officiate at the marriage of her own son.

Adrian, her other son, was the best man at his brother Stephen's wedding. Reverend Sturrock's daughter, Lisa, gave away the bride, Allison Jones.

Just as her fictional counterpart would have done, Reverend Sturrock roped all of her parishioners at St. Peter's Church into getting involved. They made the cake, decorated the church, and provided cars for the wedding party.

The vicar herself is estranged from her own husband, but no one seemed to mind.

Paul Merton and Sarah Parkinson, the couple who married themselves on the uninhabited island in the middle of the Indian Ocean, must have known something about the dangers of inviting family members to the wedding.

After all these other wedding stories, it seems that the Mertons' nuptials should be the blueprint by which all sane people should get married. They should patent that idea, or at least tape an infomercial. They'd make a fortune.

CHAPTER TEN

Tradition!

> # IF YOU DON'T KNOW
> ## where you're going,
> ## you will wind up
> # SOMEWHERE ELSE.
> —YOGI BERRA

Anytime anyone tells you anything that sounds like, "We've been doing it this way for twenty years," inhale very deeply. Soon you will smell the manure.

I'm actually not at all opposed to great wedding traditions. In fact, the sillier and more outlandishly rooted in inexplicable superstition, the more likely I am to incorporate them into my everyday life. Why wait for a wedding to make my sweetie carry me through doorways? Or walk around with a quarter in my shoe? I can think of plenty of times when an extra quarter would have come in very handy.

Much of what drives the planning and execution of typical wedding ceremonies and receptions, of course, are the family and cultural traditions handed down through the ages. We don't always know why we have to do certain things a certain way, like the groom not seeing the bride before the ceremony on the wedding day, but we know that if he does, somebody's in big trouble.

As if it weren't difficult enough to keep track of the infinite array of traditions and superstitions associated with the great art of getting married, consider the added complications that come from living in a country as ethnically diverse as the United States and the proliferation of intercultural relationships. Personally, I think these make for the most fun and memorable occasions. They're the kind of parties people talk about for decades, the stuff of blockbuster romantic comedies. But they can be a little confusing to some of the guests. Customs that make some kind of sense in whatever part of the world they originated, when imported, serve only to convince one side of the family that the other side is nuts. And then they begin to fear for the future grandchildren.

Of course, before any of us can get to the altar, there's that little matter of courtship and proposal.

In the olden days (before the 1960s), cultures all over the world put great stock in the rituals related to the selection and procurement of a suitable mate. Things have changed a lot in the years since Woodstock in virtually every place on the planet. Now we mostly do what we want, or merely nod and wink as we go through the motions. Acts that once sent our forefathers into states of near panic, like asking the girl's father for her hand in marriage, are largely forgotten. Still, such rituals do occasionally get reenacted even today, but usually after the girl has already said yes and they've given each other a test-drive . . . so to speak. Most prospective fiancés are still willing to go down on one knee as they present the diamond ring to their beloveds, but it's mostly because they're not quite sure there's any other acceptable way for a man to ask a woman to marry him.

One of the more unusual engagement rituals that has been sadly lost to modernity originated in the Philippines. In days of yore, a young man would indicate his desire to marry a girl by hurling his spear at her hut. This would let any other prospective suitors know that the girl was spoken for, and, as soon as both families agreed on the terms, she would soon belong to a man with a weapon.[9] Nowadays, a plain old engagement ring will suffice.

In modern-day Thailand, however, things are getting desperate . . . and a little schizophrenic.

Concerned that its young people are neglecting to procreate and that the country will soon be stuck with a bunch of resource-sucking old people, Singapore recently began funding educational efforts to teach young people how to go forth and multiply.

The Ngee Ann Polytechnic School has begun offering its students courses on flirting, establishing relationships, analyzing the lyrics to love songs, speed dating, and the ancient art of online chatting.

---

[9] I assume he had extra spears.

Ironically, in this morality-obsessed country (except, it seems, when it comes to the prostitution of minors), authorities were alarmed to learn that one out of four teenagers routinely plan to have sex on Valentine's Day.

Every February 14th, police and "student inspectors" undertake massive sweeps of cheap motels, shopping malls, restaurants, and public parks throughout Bangkok, searching for horny teenagers wherever they might congregate or flirt. Parents are urged to enforce strict curfews for their adolescent kids and keep a close eye on them after they get home.

There's an old story about legendary comic actor W. C. Fields that has been told, retold, and modified so many times, and claimed by so many of his purported friends, that it's difficult to know for sure if it ever actually happened in any of the ways it's been reported.

In my favorite version of the tale, Fields is lying on his deathbed, thumbing through a Bible. In walks his dear friend [fill in the blank], who exclaims, "I thought you were an atheist! What are you doing reading the Bible?!" to which Fields replies, "Looking for loopholes."

I think a lot of people do exactly that just before that *other* terrifying life-changing moment: marriage.

There's an old superstition in Puerto Rico, and probably a few other places in Latin America, that holds that if a bride's veil falls off in church as she's walking down the aisle, it's proof positive—an actual sign from God—that she's not a virgin. This is a *very* bad thing.

In the old days, the groom was permitted—even expected—to return the not-so-pure bride to her parents on the spot if such a thing should happen. This in turn paved the way for yet another long-standing tradition, the one that says that a certain portion of the bride's dowry must be set aside exclusively for the purchase of bobby pins.

A good friend of mine from Puerto Rico (who told me she'd have to kill me dead if I dared to reveal her name) practically staple-gunned her veil to her head on her wedding day. The "old days" were long gone, thank goodness, and she knew that her fiancé would never actually return her to her parents, but she also knew that if by some horrendous coincidence her veil did fall off, the gasps inside that church would have sucked another hole out of the ozone layer. It would also have given people plenty to talk about during the reception and, of course, the rest of her life; signs from God tend not to be quickly forgotten in that part of the world. Also, her good reputation would have been sullied forever by the wicked flapping of the uncharitable tongues that belonged to the very people she had loved enough to invite to her wedding.

Worst of all, my friend the bride told me, there was the very real fear that her father might be so hurt, humiliated, and/or enraged by the suggestion that his daughter's honor had been besmirched that he'd have to kill her fiancé right where he stood. Her mother, meanwhile, would have been appropriately engaged in some kind of hemorrhage. There was just too much at stake, she said. So she bought a bushel of bobby pins, a caulking gun, and a few yards of Velcro, just to be on the safe side.

"You know what the ironic thing is?" she asked me, "If that veil *had* fallen off as a sign from God, it would have been all my dumb horny boyfriend's fault anyway . . . Okay, and my own horny fault, too, but you can't tell anybody!"

"But all that happened twenty-five years ago," I reminded her. "How could anybody care now?"

She looked at me as if I were irredeemably dense. "I have a *daughter* now," she said.

After thinking about it for a moment, I managed to figure out that this must mean that, in addition to all the crazy customs, traditions, and superstitions, we also pass down to our sons and daughters all the weird fictions we have to invent for ourselves in order to survive the opinions of our alleged loved ones. I suddenly felt very sad for my friend and immediately began to wonder how many bobby pins had held *her* mother's veil down.

What's funny is that, while my friend was walking down the aisle, she actually did feel something shift on her head. Maybe it was just God playing a little trick on her. Or maybe it was psychosomatic. Who knows?

Ay-ay-ay . . . the burdens of a "virgin" bride.

Every country and culture has its own quirky way of infusing a very simple biological imperative—that of mate selection and reproduction of the species—with completely illogical rules of comportment.

Hasidic Jews, for example, believe that once a woman is married, no one but her husband should be allowed to see her hair. A woman's hair is one of the greatest outward symbols of her sensuality and femininity, traits that are deemed unbecoming—even dangerous —for an appropriately modest woman, at least according to *halacha* (Orthodox Jewish law).

> *Many Hasidic women shave their heads on their wedding night. They then go out and buy the most fabulous wigs their husbands' parents can afford and wear them the rest of their lives.*

Thank God for the loophole.

Many Hasidic women shave their heads on their wedding night. They then go out and buy the most fabulous wigs their husbands' parents can afford (traditionally, it's the groom's family who foots the bill for the *sheitel*) and wear them the rest of their lives (or until they get new ones for everyday use or special occasions). Handmade from real human hair and styled in expensive specialty shops, the wigs are very often much more beautiful and luxuriant than the woman's original head of hair.

In a 1997 interview with the *New York Times,* a woman named Suzy Berkowitz from Brooklyn spoke about her most recent purchase—a $2,000 handmade wig called the Olga— which she then took to stylist Mark Garrison on Madison Avenue in Manhattan for a shampoo and cut. The salon treatment for the wig cost her another $600.

Many younger Orthodox brides insist that their *sheitels* look exactly like their own hair did while they were single. Rifka Locker, a fourth-grade teacher from New Jersey who went to great lengths to have a wig made in the style and image of her natural hair, remarked, "No one could even tell I got married!"

The wigmakers and stylists who specialize in catering to the hair-care needs of Orthodox Jewish women do such an amazing job that you'd really have to look hard—or give a good tug—to know for sure that the woman was wearing someone else's hair, but that would be a little rude.[10]

There's an old saying among Jews: Ask twelve rabbis a question, and you'll get thirteen opinions. Rabbi Avi Weiss points out, "There can be two views, and they can be both opposite and correct." Rabbi Mayer Fund is also quoted by the *Times* as saying, "Whatever the Torah prohibits the Torah permits." This explains how Orthodox Jews are able to reconcile the seeming contradiction of a woman shaving her head

---

[10] I must admit that, since learning this, I have been absolutely helpless to keep from staring at women's heads on crowded subways. It's easier to do during rush hour if I'm standing and a woman with an exceptionally nice head of hair is seated in front of me. "Is that a wig? Is that an Olga?" I silently obsess. So if you think someone's staring at your head on the train, it's probably me. But I promise I'm not trying to be rude.

as the law requires, and then wearing a wig that is at least as beautiful as her original head of hair.

Of course, there are rabbis who disapprove of the *sheitel* altogether. Still, women are not routinely banished from their communities for choosing a wig over a babushka.

So what we have here is a group of women who will clearly go to great lengths to honor their traditions and religious teachings. They just don't want their wigs to look too "wiggy."

Who can blame them?

In India, the *bindi*—the little red dot or jewel many women wear on their foreheads—is meant to symbolize the perfect purity of marriage and femininity. In the northern part of the country, the custom of wearing a *bindi* indicates that a woman is already married. In the south, all women and girls wear them. In other parts of India, everybody wears them, even the men.

Legend has it that a *bindi* on a woman's forehead has the power to mesmerize her lover. Throughout the ages, poems and songs have been written in praise of the beautiful *bindi*, the first thing that catches an admirer's eye.

The *bindi* is also said to represent the mystic "third eye," a sort of gateway to higher consciousness. It is often associated with clairvoyance, visions, precognition, and other forms of extrasensory perception. I suppose then, on some level, it might also serve as a wife's reminder to her husband: "I've got all *three* of my eyes on you, buddy."

In the 1990s, Madonna managed to incur the scorn of nine hundred million Hindus when she took to wearing a *bindi* as a fashion accessory.

The bridal dowry is another time-honored Indian tradition. It's such an important part of the social structure there that a family's fortune can be made or broken, depending on whether they're the ones giving or receiving the dowry. In fact, many parents dread giving birth to girls, who can cost the family everything it owns when the time comes to marry them off.

For years international human rights organizations have reported all manner of drastic—often tragic—measures many families have taken to avoid having to pay a dowry to their daughters' future in-laws. For this reason the government has banned the dowry practice altogether. Not surprisingly, the laws have been largely useless in obliterating thousands of years of tradition. The groom's side of the family will often harass the bride's family until they pony up much more than the original offer.

British newspapers recently reported the case of an Indian man who attempted to extort another 8 million rupees (about $200,000) from his dearly beloved's family. The girl's parents had already handed over more than $10,000 worth of jewelry.

The young man had secretly videotaped the girl having sex with him and now threatened to post the video online if he didn't get the extra cash. The ploy backfired and earned him and his father a short stint in jail. They're both out on bail, but a court case is pending.

Every year in Swaziland, one of the smallest countries in Africa, a great festival is held in which thousands of young women compete to be selected as their king's next bride. The competition consists mostly of bare-breasted virgins in beaded necklaces and traditional Swazi skirts doing the Reed Dance. In their honor, the king orders the slaughter of a great many cows.

In 2001, King Mswati III reinstated the ancient *umchwasho* custom, which holds that no girl under the age of eighteen is allowed to have sex. He did this primarily in an effort to stem the tide of the AIDS epidemic in his country, which was hit harder than almost any other place in the world. The king figured they would try this approach for the next five years to see if placing limitations on the sex lives of teenage girls would have a measurable effect on the overall health of his people.

Umchwasho requires that virgins wear a tasseled scarf to indicate their chastity. If a man makes sexual advances at a girl wearing such a garment, she is entitled to throw her tassels onto his property and demand that his family hand over a cow.

Cow or no cow, the girls hated this custom, especially since the king was notorious for ignoring it himself. His ninth wife, after all, was a seventeen-year-old girl. There's no telling how many other cows he had to hand over in the meantime.

King Mswati finally relented to the growing criticism coming at him from all sides, in particular from his angry young female subjects, who felt they were unfairly punished by the law; no such ordinances of chastity were put on men of any age. The king rescinded *umchwasho* in August 2005, a year earlier than planned.

At that year's festival, more than twenty thousand Swazi girls registered to take part in the Reed Dance. Several hundred others from the Zulu kingdom in neighboring South Africa also came to compete for a chance at becoming the king's fourteenth wife. The king happily chose another seventeen-year-old.

Considering the enormous scale of the competition, the odds of winning it, and King Mswati's track record, I think those Swazi girls might have been better off taking that cow deal.

Clear across the continent, in the African nation of Guinea Bissau, the laws of the Balanta tribe require a woman to remain married for at least one month or until her wedding dress wears out, whichever takes longest. After that first month, she can rip the dress to shreds if she decides her husband isn't worth keeping. The law recognizes this act as a valid divorce.

Water seems to figure prominently among most of the world's wedding traditions and superstitions. For example, it is said that if it rains on your wedding day, you will shed many tears throughout your marriage. On the other hand, some cultures believe that rain portends that you'll have a lot of children. If you're Catholic, however, and you'd prefer it not to rain for either one of these reasons, you might want to put a statue of the Virgin Mary on the windowsill, facing out. This is supposed to ensure a sunny wedding day. Also, you can hang your rosary beads on a clothesline or outside of your window. If you're a Baptist, then I guess you'll just have to deal with the rain.

It is also said that, regardless of whether the skies are clear or it rains cats and dogs, if you cry on your wedding day, that will be the last time you weep over your marriage—unless you wear pearls, in which case, depending on where in the world you get married, you will either cry . . . or not cry.

In the United States, some brides believe that pearls will prevent them from crying. This is important to American women, who have been known to spend many thousands of dollars to have their faces professionally made up for their wedding day and to pay for photographers and videographers to capture every nanosecond of the happy event. Tears are simply out of the question.

However, if the bride is Mexican, every pearl in her necklace represents one horrible thing her husband will do to make her cry at some point in their marriage.

I'm not sure what happens if the bride is wearing a pearl-encrusted dress, like the one Diana Spencer wore in 1981 when she married Prince Charles. Princess Diana certainly had a lot of reasons to cry throughout her marriage, and, coincidentally, her dress was one of the pearliest in all the world's history.

The good news for most brides is that very few of them can afford a multimillion-dollar pearl-encrusted dress. Also, I don't think the curse works if the pearls are fake. So if you have your heart set on it, go ahead and wear the pearls, fake or not. You might want to check with your embassy first, about the cry/don't cry thing.

Another belief associated with the dress is that if it is torn on the bride's wedding day, the marriage will end in death.

Lucky the bride whose dress remains intact! That means her marriage will end in one of the other two possibilities: divorce or abandonment.

Who makes this stuff up?

I have a great tendency toward believing that most superstitions—wedding related or not—emerge from the most ordinary of circumstances. They all began as banal, commonsensical advice that later got twisted through multiple and repeated translations and cultural misunderstandings. Someday, a perfectly ordinary warning label such as DO NOT USE HAIR DRYER IN SHOWER will become "It is bad luck for a bride to style her hair while her butt is covered in suds."

Take, for example, the tradition of the groom carrying the bride over the threshold. It is said that custom originated when pillagers of yore stole women from the towns they were terrorizing and physically carried these kicking and screaming maidens away with them. That's kind of an awful thing to want to reenact all these enlightened centuries later.

Still, I can easily imagine that that "tradition" started in a much less offensive way, like with a klutzy new bride tripping over her own feet and killing herself and/or her husband as she walked for the first time through the door of her new house—which, by the way, he probably built for her with his own two hands and on his days off from his regular job, which more than likely had nothing to do with carpentry or architectural design. The villagers then began to advise grooms-to-be that it was probably best to *carry* their new brides through the front door while pointing out all the danger spots, at least that first time.

Then word got around. In the beginning, everyone knew why, so no one had to explain the peculiar habit of carrying an otherwise able-bodied human being a foot and a half into the house. Eventually, though, people forgot why because nobody talked about it anymore, so they just did it out of habit. And a few generations later, when people no longer remembered why the groom should carry the bride, we simply explained it away by saying, "It's tradition."

> *And a few generations later, when people no longer remembered why the groom should carry the bride, we simply explained it away by saying, "It's tradition."*

Here's another tradition I just don't buy: tying tin cans to the back of the getaway car, purportedly to scare away evil spirits. This sounds an awful lot like something a bunch of frat boys would do to startle sleeping dogs and babies. More significantly, however, it's a deliberate ploy to make everybody look.

I bet the first guy who did it drove all over town yelling, "Guess who's getting *some* tonight!!!" As the tradition caught on—and surely spread like wildfire—the explanation became superfluous. Now people just do it, and nobody quite knows why.

Some people might argue that my frat-boy theory is full of holes. They would cite historical references from as far back as ancient Egypt and Rome to prove that tying things to the back of a moving vehicle is a perfectly rational thing to do.

In the Middle Ages, for example, people would bang on pots and pans after the wedding ceremony because, as anyone will tell you, despite the fact that evil spirits have the power to kill or maim a bride, they are terribly frightened of loud noises. One would think that the noise would alert the evil spirits to the exact location of the bride and groom, but apparently that was not the case.

In these more illuminated times, very few people show up for a wedding with their old pots and pans. The medieval tradition was modified so that someone in the wedding party is put in charge of tying tin cans to the car. And so it is that the ancient tradition lives on today, and we hardly ever hear of newlyweds being killed by evil spirits anymore. We do occasionally hear about the dangers of creating sparks so close to the gas tank.

Instead of tin cans, some newlyweds end up with old shoes tied to the back of the car. This is, of course, a less obnoxious way of calling attention to oneself and, in the end, somewhat more civilized.

Shoes were significant at weddings in ancient Egypt. When the father of the bride gave away his daughter, he also handed the groom the girl's sandals. This symbolized the father transferring authority over the girl to her new husband.

Sounds to me like he's really saying, "Take her *and* her shoes. Make sure she can't walk back."

The British, and the Anglo-Saxons from whom they descended, also had wedding customs involving footwear. In the centuries before people were properly introduced into polite society, they would throw their shoes at a newly married couple. Tradition held that great luck would be bestowed upon the shoe-thrower if he or she hit the bride, the groom, or whatever form of transportation they were using.

Things must have gotten out of hand at some point along the way when, hundreds of years later in America, the State of Colorado outlawed the practice of throwing shoes at the bride and groom. The law is still on the books to this day.

Thankfully, in the centuries since, the British have developed the most impeccable manners on Earth. They now consider it vulgar to throw one's shoes at married people, their horses, or their carriages. Instead, in some parts of England, they now wait for the bride to arrive at the reception, and then throw a cake plate at her head. They are, of course, very careful to miss.

Here's the only wedding tradition that makes perfect sense to me: the bride carrying a bouquet of flowers. They are beautiful to behold, create a wonderful contrast against a white wedding dress, and are effective in hiding the occasional "baby bump" from the cameras.

The origins of the bouquet, however, are firmly rooted in practicality. Rather than flowers, they used to be made of fragrant herbs and spices, such as thyme and garlic. This was done to mask the unbearable stench of body odor. A long time ago, people rarely bathed, not even for special occasions.

The wedding cake business in the United States is a multi-billion-dollar industry. For a 2006 bridal show in California, a cake designer joined forces with a Beverly Hills jeweler to create a single diamond-studded cake priced at more than $20 million. The average couple, however, will spend considerably less on a cake, somewhere in the neighborhood of $500.

In America and in many other places in the world, it is customary for the groom to feed the first piece of cake to his bride. She then feeds him a bit of the confection. This is meant to symbolize the first act of caring and nurturing between the newly married couple.

At almost every American wedding, however, the bride and groom smear each other's faces with the cake—to a greater or lesser degree, depending on the couple. The mini food fight, then, would appear to be a more realistic depiction of what lies ahead for them both.

Tracey and John O'Donnell got a little carried away during this part of their wedding reception in 1993. They were both ar-rested for disturbing the peace when the playful smearing of the cake got a little out of hand. Tracey said John fed her the cake a little too roughly, so she retaliated. The ritual turned into a fistfight.

The top layer of the wedding cake is also a matter of great controversy, depending on which side of the Atlantic you call home. In the United States, the couple is supposed to freeze the top tier of the cake and eat it on their first anniversary. In Britain, you're supposed to save it for the christening of your first child.

Old freezer-burned cake. What a horrible thing to feed a baby.

The Iranians incorporate a much more sensual feeding tradition into their weddings. Instead of smearing cake all over their faces at the reception, the couple licks honey from each other's fingers during the ceremony. This is done to ensure that their life together begins sweetly.

Sadly, this tradition backfired horribly for a couple getting married in 2001 in Qazvin, a city in the northwestern region of that country. Along with the honey, the groom sucked the fake fingernail off his bride's hand and choked to death right where he stood.

Perhaps because I've never been to China, or because I've only ever seen pictures of Asian weddings on television and magazines, ceremonies in that part of the world seem extraordinarily beautiful and elaborate to me. I don't know what they're saying to each other or why it looks as if somebody's head would get chopped off if anyone made a mistake, but it appeals very much to my love of ritual.

I find it a little sad that, as the cultural borders of our world become less rigid—which ordinarily I would say is an *excellent* thing—the so-called Western traditions are slowly infiltrating the sensibilities of brides all over the place, but in particular in Asia.

The traditional Chinese wedding banquet, for example, is of little interest to many modern couples. They prefer instead to mimic what they see in Hollywood movies—an outdoor party on a beautifully landscaped lawn, a candlelight dinner for six or seven hundred, or a reception that begins with the wedding party parachuting into the crowd of waiting guests.

Some traditions hold fast, though. Done the old way, the Chinese wedding is comprised of three parts: (1) the groom picks up the bride at her family's house, (2) the couple goes to the wedding location to have their pictures taken, and (3) they have the banquet. Before the invention of the camera, I guess they had somebody slap a few quick watercolors on a sheet of rice paper for phase 2.

Part of the ritual of picking the bride up from her parents' house involves the family pretending to put up a fight. They will not relinquish the daughter until the groom ponies up some money wrapped in the traditional red silk pouches.

In the modern version of the traditional Chinese wedding, the groom must also answer a series of embarrassing questions, *a la* dumb American game show.

Modern Chinese brides are also quite keen on marrying on Valentine's Day. Perhaps this is appealing on many levels. In the West, red is the color associated with that holiday. It is also considered the luckiest color in Chinese culture.

However, no matter how modern a Chinese couple wants to be, they just can't make themselves walk down the aisle on anything but a red carpet. A white carpet or runner is what is used for funerals in China.

For better or for worse, the old traditions are fading. The greatest proof of this is in the wedding package offered by the Shanghai Extreme Sports Centre. Brides and grooms who desire a complete departure from the traditional celebration can request a service called the Flying Couple. In this ghastly event, the couple is tied together with bungee cords, thrown from a considerable height, and then allowed to dangle together for a little while. The experience is an allegory for the life that lies ahead for them as married people.

The people of Thailand have also come to embrace Valentine's Day as a lovers' holiday. Like the Chinese, many Thai soon-to-be brides and grooms eagerly await the fourteenth of February to celebrate their weddings in any number of spectacular ways. Some choose ceremonies conducted on mountain cliffs or under water. Others take their vows in hot-air balloons floating high above their cities and villages. Particularly superstitious couples flock to Bangkok's "District of Love" on Valentine's Day to register their marriages in the city office located there.

Beloved Princess Galyani Vadhana unwittingly put a damper on the festivities in 2008 when she dropped dead at the age of eighty-four just after New Year's Day. The required one hundred days of mourning meant that all public celebrations, including weddings, would have to be cancelled or postponed.

Oh, well. There's always next year.

The renewal of wedding vows is an increasingly popular tradition, especially on the occasion of a significant anniversary like the tenth, twenty-fifth, or any other one ending in zero. Some couples recommit to one another to mark the big milestones, or after one spouse has finally forgiven the other for some horrible breach of etiquette or unspeakable transgression.

Some people should just leave well enough alone, like Fabiana Reyes and Elmo Hernandez of Port Chester, New York.

Fabiana and Elmo were married in 1986 in a simple civil ceremony but always regretted not having had the all-out church wedding and grand reception. Twenty-two years later, they finally got their wish. Their twenty-one-year-old daughter Helen stood by as her parents renewed their commitment to each other before God.

At the reception, Fabiana was somewhat disappointed that the band had not played live music at St. Peter's Episcopal Church, as she requested. So she went into a screaming rage and destroyed the band's conga drums. She also trashed one of the sound system's speakers.

The police arrived soon after and arrested Fabiana. Elmo and Helen stepped in to try to save her from the mean, heartless cops. The officers zapped them both with a stun gun and loaded them into the police cruisers. They were charged with interfering with Fabiana's arrest.

Fabiana spent the next six days in jail. She later paid the band an additional $1,500 for their trouble. Elmo and Helen were fined $250 each.

I wish I knew what part of our psyche or emotional makeup draws us to the repetition of age-old practices, whether or not we understand them. There's so much silliness we'll accept and repeat without question just because everyone who came before us did it. Somebody shouts, "Jump the broom!" or "Throw the flowers!" and we do it, without stopping for a single moment to think about the fact that this act has absolutely no practical purpose and is totally illogical.

This, more than anything, is what separates us from the animals.

CHAPTER ELEVEN

If I'd Had a Hammer

> Marriage is like putting
> your hand into a bag
> of snakes in the hope of
> **PULLING OUT AN EEL.**
> —*Leonardo da Vinci*

It's a good thing my ex-husband wasn't home the day I decided to throw him out. I might otherwise be writing this on the walls of my cozy little jail cell, or in crayon in the community room of some nuthouse.

Anyone who has ever been in love has a story or two of his or her own to prove that love makes you do crazy things. More accurately, it's the *end* of love that can send ordinarily decent, law-abiding people barreling headfirst into the land of the criminally insane. Fortunately, for most of us it's a short visit.

I've always been rather proud of the way in which my ex-husband and I handled the end of our marriage. There was no fighting over the rightful ownership of a ten-year-old toaster that produced limp, untoasted bread on one side and blue sparks out of the other. Neither did we spend endless months in front of a lawyer, quibbling over the value or origins of a faux-copper-bottomed lidless pot neither one of us could remember purchasing, receiving as a gift, or inheriting from a previous failed relationship. In the end, it was all rather civilized.

There was, however, a ten-minute interval that was anything but civilized.

I woke up one bright, sunny morning in March with a sick sort of feeling that something wasn't right.

I'd never snooped on his computer before, but a nagging little voice kept suggesting that maybe the time had come for me to start. It didn't take long at all for me to find all the evidence I'd ever need in a court of law. From the looks of it, I should have snooped a lot sooner.

In a span of time just a few minutes long, I managed to empty the entire house of every single item that looked

like him, smelled like him, or might otherwise have ever been owned by him. It took me all of ten minutes.

I remember going up and down the stairs many times, careening in and out of rooms like a pinball racking up bonus points, carrying massive armloads of clothes, books, computers, CDs, and generally anything I knew for a fact didn't belong exclusively to me. I made quite a lovely heap in the garage, squarely on the spot where his car should have been at seven o'clock in the morning. Every time I dumped another armload in that not-supposed-to-be-empty parking space, I got just a little bit crazier.

Several months before, the UPS man had delivered a NordicTrack treadmill to our doorstep. It had arrived unassembled and in two separate boxes, each of which was much too heavy for me to lift by myself. I had to wait for my husband to come home to bring it into the house. It took the two of us to lift each of those boxes one by one and drag them a few inches inside. We put the horrid contraption together, set it up in a corner of the room closest to the foyer, and then left it there, presumably forever. There was no way we would ever be able to move it anywhere else. We agreed that, when the time came, we'd sell it right along with the house, throw it in as a bonus.

It was that treadmill that now crowned the top of the heap in the garage. I had lifted it up over my head, carried it through the kitchen—where I had recently had new flooring put in and would be goddamned if I was going to let this monstrous thing scratch it—and thrown it on top of everything else already piled there.

At 7:10 a.m., I stood before my mountain of refuse, a panting, snorting, growling animal, fingers splayed into claws, smoke coming out of my hair. I gazed with dismay upon everything that had once been "his stuff," and wished there was more. I was Carrie at the prom, Joan Crawford in the rosebushes with the hedge clippers, Mrs. Peacock in the kitchen with a lead NordicTrack. I am certain that I was, at the end of my love, the very picture of ape-shit crazy.

Ten minutes. I emptied our house of half of its contents in ten minutes.

No one will ever convince me that there is a more powerful chemical agent in the universe than rage-induced adrenaline.

> *No one will ever convince me that there is a more powerful chemical agent in the universe than rage-induced adrenaline.*

I left him messages on his cell phone and at his office, and then decided to go for a little drive. For three hours I muttered under my breath, "If I were a scorned woman worth my salt, I'd have thrown all of his stuff out into the middle of the street for all of our neighbors— the normal people—to see. I should be waiting for him at the end of the cul-de-sac at the top of the heap, straddling the fricking NordicTrack with a gas can in one hand and a lit match in the other."

Upon my return, I saw an enormous rental truck parked in front of the house. He had, apparently, received my messages. The lovely heap, however, was still on the garage floor.

I suspect he intended to call my bluff, perhaps try to persuade me to give him yet another chance. One look into my eyeballs, which were still jiggling wildly in their sockets, convinced him otherwise. I stomped into the house, ripped a few sheets from the Yellow Pages, got back into my car, and went to find a lawyer. I ended up picking some guy whose last name started with *A*.

After that, everything was fine.

The settlement was negotiated quickly and without argument, no silly battles over ancient toasters or lidless pots. We agreed to part as friends.

To me, that meant simply that if I saw him crossing the street, I would not run him over with my car.

And so it remains to this day.

I told this story to my friend Ernie. I half expected him to run away screaming, too scared to be my friend anymore. Instead, he said, "I know exactly what you mean." And then he told me about his own Carrie-Crawford-Peacock moment.

Ernie was brought up right, taught never to raise his hand to a woman. He's a big guy, very tall and a little scary looking, but surprisingly calm and easygoing. He reserves most of his outrage for street punks and bullies, who, fortunately for us all, tend to stay out of his way without much prompting. All he has to do is show up.

"But then one day, it happened," he said. "From the moment I got home from work until I finally put an end to it, my wife just wouldn't stop pushing buttons. Push, push, poke, poke, jab, nag, push. I really wanted to deck her." Instead, Ernie raised two enormous, vibrating fists in the air, made some kind of feral noise, and punched himself hard, right in the temple. The blow spun him into the doorjamb, out of the room, and into the hall, where he fell with a house-rattling thud.

In all of his rage, he had managed to knock himself unconscious.

"That's when I knew it was over," he said.

I tried hard not to laugh.

And we shouldn't laugh at these stories. They are often very painful, harsh reminders of a difficult past.

So I'll tell you just a few more.

For some couples, the marriage never truly ends, not even after a divorce. All the rage and old hurts remain as fresh as a head of lettuce in the fridge's crisper.

In November 2007, Ryann Jean Stafford, from Meridian, Ohio, got into a very ugly argument with her ex-husband, probably over his new girlfriend. It ended with Ryann throwing things at him as he ran out of his own house. When he was farther away than she could throw, she set fire to the bison head mounted on his living room wall.

Ryann may end up serving ten years in prison for third-degree arson, but we should probably give her some credit for choosing an inanimate object as the target for her rage. And she probably knows that. Still, she appears to have derived a certain satisfaction from her little escapade. I'm not sure how else to explain the creepy smirk on her face and the wild-eyed look she was wearing when they took her mug shot.

Jason Fife, from Norristown, Pennsylvania, had a similar idea when he found out his wife was having an affair in 2006.

He mailed the severed head of a cow to the home of his wife's lover. The cow had a puncture wound in its skull.

Jason told the police that he got the cow's head from a butcher shop and mailed it while it was still frozen. No one was suspicious of the package . . . until it began to ooze blood after sitting in the warm June sun on the victim's doorstep.

Jason was sentenced to two years of probation and fifty hours of community service. He and his wife have since reconciled. No word on what became of her lover.

Amanda Moya's boyfriend was smart enough to have had her arrested the last time she beat him up, but not enough to sit with her in his underwear in his Albuquerque home to watch a porn movie.

As the flick began to roll on that night in April 2008, Amanda thought that the resemblance between her boyfriend and the star of the X-rated video was not coincidental. She soon became convinced that she was actually watching her own dearly beloved right there on the television screen. So she attacked him.

The boyfriend managed to escape, but not before Amanda cut his face, bit his torso, and threatened to kill

him with a knife. He ran out of the house and called 911 on his cell phone as he continued to run down the street in his boxer shorts. "She almost shanked me and everything!" he screamed at the operator. "She put the fucking knife right under my throat!" The 911 dispatcher advised him to keep running.

With Amanda still hot on his tail and brandishing the knife, the boyfriend was able to flag down the police cruiser that was headed toward his house. A sheriff's deputy arrested Amanda at the scene and charged her with aggravated assault and battery. Charges of child abuse were tacked on a bit later; Amanda had left her eight-month-old baby alone in the house while she chased her boyfriend down the street.

I can relate completely to Emma Thomason, from White-haven, England, who had a similar need to see all of her fiancé's belongings heaped into one neat little pile.

Emma got into an argument with Jason Wilson, her partner of seven years and the father of her two children. While he was away one day in May 2007, she filled his van up with everything he owned—clothes, music recordings, DVDs— then drove the van to a nearby harbor and sank the whole kit and caboodle.

She was charged with aggravated vehicle-taking without consent but was released on bail. Jason has avoided telling Emma that the wedding is definitely off.

In December 2006, Dean Kuehnen Jr. asked his dearly beloved, Andria Castellano, to marry him. To show just how much she meant to him, he gave her a 3.23-carat diamond ring worth nearly $49,000.

By September 2007, the wedding was off, but not the ring.

Andria still has it, and Dean wants it back. Andria says she'd sooner blow the diamond ring to smithereens than hand it over to Dean. So Dean filed a case in New York State Court and is suing her for the ring, in addition to all of his legal fees and expenses.

The twenty-one-year-old ex-fiancée is not giving it up without a fight. The case is still pending.

There is one woman who took things much further than I could ever imagine, and who clearly felt no need to take out her rage on her ex-boyfriend's things when the man himself was standing right in front of her.

Amanda Monti, from Liverpool, England, once had a "long-term but open relationship" with Geoffrey Jones. It ended on relatively good terms in May 2004.

About a year later, the two met up again after a party. They went with some friends back to Geoffrey's house. Amanda made a few suggestive advances, all of which Geoffrey rejected. This so enraged Amanda that she pulled his pants down, ripped off his left testicle with her bare hands, and then tried to eat it. Unable to swallow it, she spat it out. One of the friends picked it up and handed it back to Geoffrey, saying, "This is yours."

> *This so enraged Amanda that she pulled his pants down, ripped off his left testicle with her bare hands, and then tried to eat it. Unable to swallow it, she spat it out.*

In a letter to the court, Amanda said she was very sorry and insisted that she was "in no way a violent person." Judge Charles James observed, "This is a very serious injury," then sentenced her to two and a half years in prison.

Michael Moylan, from Port St. Lucie, Florida, was awakened by a terrible headache in the middle of an otherwise ordinary night in the summer of 2007. The pain was so severe that he woke his wife, April, and asked her to take him to the emergency room.

Michael should have suspected something was fishy as soon as April put the car in motion. She drove very slowly, making full stops at every corner even though it was the middle of the night and there was no one else on the road inside their upscale gated community at four o'clock in the morning. And rather than leaving through the main entrance, she steered the car through a construction entrance.

Doctors examined Michael and quickly found the cause of his headache: There was a thirty-eight-caliber bullet lodged behind his right ear.

Michael and his doctors turned to look at April Moylan, who spun around and ran in an attempt to flee the emergency room. She was caught and turned over to the police. She later told the sheriff's deputies that she had shot her husband by accident. Unconvinced this was a mistake, the deputies placed April under arrest.

Michael was released from the hospital after only a couple of days and, amazingly, walked away on his own two legs. The bullet, however, is still in his head.

Michael later told investigators that he confronted his wife about the shooting, and that she confessed to him that she had done it on purpose but did not give a reason.

He made her sleep on the couch that night.

I bet Ken Slaby, from Pennsylvania, wished he'd never fallen asleep on Gail O'Toole's couch. Ken was Gail's ex-boyfriend.

In 1999, Gail and Ken had been pretty seriously involved. Ken claimed that he loved her then and was devastated when she broke things off after only ten months. He got over it soon enough, though. A couple of months later, he had found someone new.

When that relationship ended, Ken and Gail hooked up again and attempted a reconciliation. Or so Ken was led to believe.

One night, Gail picked Ken up at his house and drove him back to her place. After Ken fell asleep, Gail got busy.

She superglued his penis to his stomach and his testicle to his leg. Then she glued the crack of his ass shut. And as a finishing touch, she painted his head and face with nail polish.

Then she woke him up and told him to get the hell out of her house.

Ken had to walk a mile down the road to call 911 from a pay phone. It took him a very long time to get there.

The emergency room nurses tried all sorts of solvents to try to dissolve the superglue. Nothing worked. So they had to pry him apart the hard way.

Gail explained to the police officer who came to arrest her that that's the way she and Ken always had sex. The cop didn't buy it.

Gail was convicted of simple assault and sentenced to six months' probation for taking this bit of twisted revenge on poor old Ken.

In 2005, Slaby won a civil suit in which Gail was ordered to pay him $46,200 in damages.

If somebody had to rip my Crazy Glued butt cheeks apart to restore a proper crack to my ass, I know I'd want a hell of a lot more than $46,200.

There's a man named Remington Watson who tried to avoid jail time some other way when his rage got completely out of hand. When his wife, Jocelyn, asked him for a divorce, he hit her over the head with a brick, which killed her. He then got into his car wearing nothing but his underwear and slammed it into a parked gasoline tanker in attempt to turn this episode into a murder-suicide. As luck would have it, he survived. Apparently, gasoline tankers don't always explode like they do in the movies. Watson was sentenced to eighteen years in prison.

Some couples don't need to be married very long to develop that sort of rage. Scott McKie and Victoria Anderson were married for ninety minutes when all hell broke loose.

The couple, from Manchester, England, tied the knot in December 2004. During the wedding reception, Scott offered a rather tasteless toast to the bridesmaids. Deeply offended, Victoria picked up a hat stand and hurled it across the room like a javelin, aiming directly at Scott. Fortunately for them both, she missed, but police were called to the scene nonetheless.

When the officers arrived, Scott head-butted one of them and punched another in the face. He was immediately thrown in jail.

Victoria stayed at the party, announcing to the guests that this was now a celebration of her impending divorce.

Scott was sentenced to sixty hours of community service and given a night curfew for the next three months. Victoria was let off with a warning.

Teresa Brown and Mark Allerton celebrated their nuptials in Scotland in the traditional blowout way. Big dress, big party, big hair . . . the works.

The reception was in full swing in the ballroom of the Hilton Treetops Hotel in Aberdeen when Mark and Teresa stole away to their hotel room upstairs. A few minutes later, they got into a terrible fight, which ended only after Teresa took off one of her stiletto heels and drove it pointy-part-first into her new husband's head.

Mark managed to get away and ran to the front desk clutching a blood-soaked towel to his head.

Police arrived to find Teresa sitting on the floor, surrounded by broken glass. She was arrested and spent her honeymoon weekend in a jailhouse cell.

Mark and Teresa are still together, but only because of the therapy.

Things didn't go so well at the wedding of a Saudi Arabian man and his new wife in the summer of 2003. The bride's brother took a snapshot of the two immediately after the ceremony, which so enraged the groom that he pounced on his new brother-in-law and prepared to beat him silly. He was restrained and dissuaded from assaulting the man, so the groom did the next best thing. He ended the marriage on the spot by shouting "I divorce you!" at his wife the required three times.

Adrienne Samen, on the other hand, an eighteen-year-old Connecticut bride, did not count on any of her wedding pictures being mug shots. Adrienne apparently tried to calm her wedding jitters with a little too much booze.

During her August 2003 reception, she got into a heated discussion with employees of the Mill on the River restaurant. According to the police, Adrienne "flipped out" and began yelling at everyone before she stormed outside. When officers approached the bride, she cursed at them and gave them the finger.

The officers put Adrienne into the police cruiser and hauled her off to jail. On the ride there, she kicked the inside of the car's door and window and tried to bite a cop when he attempted to restrain her with a seat belt.

Things didn't get better at the South Windsor police headquarters, where Adrienne refused to cooperate with the officers trying to book her. She was tossed into a jail cell, Cinderella gown and all, and was given a few hours to cool down. She was charged with criminal mischief and breach of peace, and released after posting $1,000 bail.

Not all tales of love gone bad end in temporary insanity or imprisonment. Larry Star is an example of grace under estrangement, and teaches us all the value of humor as a way of finding closure.

In April 2004, Larry placed an advertisement on the online auction Web site eBay. It read as follows: "For Sale: One Slightly Used Size 12 Wedding Gown. Only worn twice: Once at the wedding and once for these pictures."

Larry Star found his ex-wife's wedding dress in the attic shortly after their divorce. His sister convinced him that he should try to sell it. It was a pretty dress, after all, and it had cost him $1,200. His former father-in-law had promised to reimburse him for it but never made good on the offer.

Larry figured he had nothing left to lose with regard to this curdled union, so he squeezed himself into the dress, had his picture taken, and posted the photo with the ad. He was willing to let any lucky girl have it for a couple of Seattle Mariner's tickets and a six-pack of beer.

A bidding frenzy soon ensued. When the auction ended on April 28, 2004, the winning bid had reached $3,850. The ad had been viewed 5.8 billion times.

The buyer ultimately backed out and Larry still owns the dress, but the ad brought him quite a bit of notoriety. He has appeared on nationally syndicated television news programs and has performed onstage as a stand-up comic, always wearing the dress.

Ian Usher did Larry Star one better: When his marriage ended, he decided to put his whole life up for sale on eBay.

The forty-four-year-old Australian man's auction, which went live in June 2008, included a house valued at just under $400,000, all of his clothes, his car, a motorcycle, a Jet Ski, a spa, his entire collection of friends, and a two-week trial run at his job at a rug store in Perth.

On his Web site, ALife4Sale.com, Ian writes, "I have had enough of my life! I don't want it any more! You can have it if you like!"

Ian's ex-wife suspects he has lost his mind. Lucky for them both, she no longer has a say in the matter.

Ian fared much better than Larry Star in his auction, but was still disappointed with the result. The winning bid was not quite $384,000. Ian wouldn't go into details about what he'd do next, but acknowledged that the sum would do nicely to fund a brand new start.

Nothing makes us feel more human than love. It follows, then, that nothing can unleash the baser aspects of our nature faster than the end of love. We are impelled to destroy that which would deprive us of our humanity.

I know people who have walked away from relationships with barely a shrug. None of those people were walking away from love. On one or two occasions, I've been one of those people.

I also know it makes us crazy to lose at love. We forget everything we've learned as civilized people and turn into some primal version of ourselves. If nobody ever taught us manners, if we never learned self-control, maybe that's who we'd really be. We'd be just like those monkeys in the zoo that throw poop at people who annoy them.

The one great thing about us having risen a step or two above poop throwing is that, more often than not, we turn that destructive rage against the ex's things, and not the actual ex. It gets the job done, gives us closure, and generally involves a lot less jail time. I think we should find a way of working that into some kind of legislation.

CHAPTER TWELVE

Heaven Help Us

> You can put wings
> on a pig, but that
> DOESN'T MAKE
> IT AN EAGLE.
> —BILL CLINTON

There are people who have made a career out of preaching morality in their underwear. Politicians and televangelists are particularly adept at this. They're easy targets, of course. Too easy sometimes. But that's what makes this so much fun.

When Congress first authorized the Federal Communication Commission (FCC) to grant broadcast licenses, one of the requirements imposed on radio stations was that they include programming "in the public interest." Most radio station owners took this to mean that they could sell time to members of the clergy so they could talk about religion to their hearts' content, and that that was as good a public interest as any to satisfy that requirement. For the most part, the FCC went along with the plan.

Immediately, thousands of preachers and ministers all over the country beat a path to their local radio stations, eagerly seeking air time. The stations quickly realized that they needed to think things through a little more.

Too many men of the cloth got a little too carried away, such as Father Charles Coughlin, who used much of his program time to spread a hateful word or two about blacks and Jews.

By the time television entered the realm of mass communication in the 1950s, broadcasters had a much better handle on the situation. By then, the practice was to give time away for free—not to sell it—to "faith groups" that represented larger segments of their communities. The FCC gave the broadcasters public interest credit for this unpaid time. However, the broadcasters tended to define these groups rather narrowly and routinely excluded those on the outer fringes of passionate discourse, such as fundamentalists and evangelicals.

So in 1960, the FCC stepped in yet again and said that radio and television stations could *sell* air time to religious groups or individual preachers and still get credit for setting aside a certain number of hours for programming in the public interest.

By 1977, more than 90 percent of all religious programming was being paid for by evangelicals on television—hence the term "televangelist"—who in turn were getting more than enough money to pay for air time from their congregations out there in TV land. It was like having a self-replenishing bank account that just kept growing and growing. The money they raked in made millionaires out of former tent-revival preachers and carnival sideshow barkers. Corruption was not far behind.

Jim Bakker, along with his severely mascaraed wife, Tammy Faye, created the television ministry called Praise the Lord, or PTL. By 1987, PTL claimed more than thirteen million subscribers and assets surpassing $175 million. It was the biggest thing ever to hit the Amen Circuit. It was also the first to fall from grace in a really big way.

A church secretary by the name of Jessica Hahn changed everything for Jim and Tammy Faye.

The mousy twenty-one-year-old alleged that, in December 1980, Jim Bakker and another preacher named John Fletcher drugged and raped her. She claimed that she later overheard Bakker ask someone else in the room, "Did you get her, too?"

Bakker vehemently denied that he had ever participated in a gang rape. Years later, as Jessica's true character began to speak rather loudly for itself, it seemed unlikely that the incident was in fact a rape, as she had claimed. Many people doubted that it had happened at all. There was no doubt, however, that there had been some serious consensual canoodling going on between Jim and Jessica. Jim himself would later confirm this.

According to Jessica, the ordeal had lasted about fifteen minutes, the standard time allotment for fame in America. Soon afterward, however, she got over the horror of that experience by posing nude for *Playboy*, making porn movies, and doing lots of media interviews—all of which paid handsomely for all the gory details she could stand to reveal or make up as she went along.

As the scandal broke and the Bakkers' marriage fell apart along with the television ministry, Tammy Faye was quoted as saying, "I'm glad Jessica Hahn is so ugly, because now I don't feel so bad."

So Jessica took some of her newfound wealth and arranged to undergo extensive plastic surgery and some serious cosmetic dentistry. She now only barely resembles the rather plain but normal-looking human being she once was. But she moved to Beverly Hills, where, it is rumored, nobody looks like a normal human being anymore.

As for Jim Bakker, he was given the outrageously punitive sentence of forty-five years in prison for misappropriation of PTL funds, which included more than a quarter of a million dollars he gave Jessica Hahn to keep her big mouth shut. Jessica took the money and blabbed anyway.

The financial collapse of Bakker's evangelical dream child led to the ultimate demise of the enterprises once known as PTL, but which will forever be remembered as "Pay the Lady" in certain less respectful circles.

Jim was released from prison after only five years, but nothing would ever be the same for him. While he was in jail, Tammy Faye divorced him and married a real estate mogul. Jessica Hahn didn't have much use for him anymore, either—not that he would have drunk from that well again. But he does have a new television program in Branson, Missouri. Maybe *The Jim Bakker Show* will work out a little better for him this time.

Even more outrageous than the PTL debacle was the sex scandal that brought down that other pioneering televangelist, Jimmy Lee Swaggart.

Swaggart is a first cousin of cousin-marrying rock 'n' roll legend Jerry Lee Lewis. Maybe that doesn't mean anything. Or maybe that should have been our first clue.

During one famously indignant TV rant about the evils of homosexuality, Swaggart proclaimed, "I'm trying to find the correct name for it . . . this utter absolute, asinine, idiotic stupidity of men marrying men . . . I've never seen a man in my life I wanted to marry. And I'm gonna be blunt and plain; if one ever looks at me like that, I'm gonna kill him and tell God he died."

In one of those lovely ironic twists of fate that I find so utterly irresistible, it was Swaggart who first accused Jim Bakker of "immoral conduct" and exposed his affair with Jessica Hahn. Just a few months later, another TV preacher named Martin Gorman, whom Swaggart was also accusing of sexual misconduct and other atrocities, hired an investigator to follow Swaggart. The private eye followed him all the way to a seedy Louisiana motel, where Jimmy was raising a little hell with a prostitute.

It was only after officials from the Assemblies of God Church were shown photos of Jimmy and his gal-for-the-hour that he went on the air to give his now-infamous "I have sinned against God . . . I have sinned against you" speech, with his face covered in all manner of tears and nasal secretions. His multimillion-dollar television ministry tanked immediately afterward.

A fitting end, some would say, yet he was true to his nature. That prostitute was not a man.

By the time evangelical minister Ted Haggard's affair with his homosexual methamphetamine-procuring lover became public in 2006, the American public was so inured to such stories that we could barely manage an "Oh God, what now" as we watched the story unfold in our newspapers and television screens.

In the 1980s, Haggard founded what would become a fourteen-thousand-member megachurch in Colorado Springs called the New Life Church. Mike Jones, of Denver, made his affair with Haggard public as soon as he tuned his TV to the right channel one day and discovered that the man to whom he was supplying sex and drugs was an avid crusader against gay rights and who loudly condemned the homosexual "lifestyle."

Of course, Haggard denied it all at first. Then he said Jones was his masseuse. Then he admitted having asked Jones for drugs once, but said he didn't actually take them. In the end, he found himself standing before his wife, his five children, and all fourteen thousand members of his congregation, saying, "The fact is I am guilty of sexual immorality. And I take responsibility for the entire problem. I am a deceiver and a liar. There's a part of my life that is so repulsive and dark that I have been warring against it for all of my adult life."

I almost felt sorry for Ted Haggard. This was clearly a deeply troubled man whose inability or unwillingness to believe in a more compassionate God led to the destruction of so many lives, not just his own. Here was a man who gleefully encouraged the married members of his congregation to revel in their own sex lives. The New Life Church was full of overjoyed legally wed horny people who claimed to be getting it on almost every day, praise the Lord. The only one who could have been happier than Haggard over this was God himself.

Maybe the next time Haggard starts a megachurch, he'll build one with wider doors. And no closets.

The Cathedral of the Holy Spirit at Chapel Hill Harvester Church in Decatur, Georgia, was once a ten-thousand-member megachurch with twenty-four pastors, an archbishop, and its own media empire. With the 10 percent tithes the church required of its members, it was also able to build a Bible college, a couple of schools, and a $12 million sanctuary that spans an area roughly the size of a football field.

That was in the time before the troubles.

By the end of 2007, membership had dwindled to about 1,500, and the eighteen remaining pastors worked mostly on a volunteer basis. The Bible college and television ministry also faded into history, all thanks to the allegations of sexual hanky-panky hurled at octogenarian archbishop Earl Paulk and several other of the cathedral's men of God.

A court-ordered paternity test forced the archbishop to reveal that the current senior pastor, D. E. Paulk, was not only his nephew, but also his son. Thirty-five years before, the archbishop had had an affair with his sister-in-law, which resulted in the birth of this nephew/son. But that wasn't even close to the end of this story.

Several female church members and former employees of the megachurch came forward to denounce the archbishop and other church officials for having coerced them into sexual liaisons by telling them that it was their only path to salvation. One of the women, Mona Brewer, sued Earl Paulk, his brother Don Paulk, and the cathedral itself in 2006. At the deposition, the archbishop swore that Mona was the only woman with whom he had ever had sex outside of his marriage. That's when they did the paternity test and proved otherwise. Many more lawsuits and public accusations soon followed.

"It was a necessary evil to bring us back to God-consciousness," said nephew/son D. E. Paulk. I'm not quite sure that very many of the 8,500 former members took much comfort in that little platitude.

The archbishop's accusers and many other members of the church no longer congregate at the cathedral. They meet instead in the online support group started by Jan Royston, who turned in her membership card in 1992.

Unless you're a member of the Thorington Road Baptist Church in Montgomery, Alabama (and if you are, you probably shouldn't be reading this wicked little book), you may not have heard of the Reverend Gary Aldridge. He didn't have a fancy TV show or a big sparkly megachurch, but he was a good friend of Jerry Falwell's, and maybe that's as close to fame as he should have gotten.

But no. Alas, no.

Reverend Aldridge made international news in June 2007 when the unfortunate Christian minister died all alone in his home. He was found on the floor, hog-tied, and clad in an unforgettable *ensemble.* He was wearing two wet suits—one with suspenders, one without—rubberized underwear, diving gloves, diving slippers, two ties, five belts, eleven straps, and a diver's face mask. The only thing missing was a snorkel.

When the coroner finished peeling him out of this unimaginable getup, he found yet another little surprise: a dildo firmly ensconced deep in the reverend's ass.

The dildo was wearing a condom.

This is the most extreme case of safe sex I've ever heard.

Former governor Jim McGreevey of New Jersey recently enrolled in the seminary. After a lifetime in politics, he decided he'd be happier serving God as an Episcopal priest than as President of the United States, which was his original career choice.

Leading up to all of this was a series of events so bizarre that it could only have taken place within that realm of the universe where religion meets politics in all the wrong ways.

Let's start at the beginning: McGreevey's first marriage was to a Canadian woman named Kari Schulz. This union produced a daughter but ended in divorce. Next he married Portuguese-born Dina Matos and had another daughter. That marriage also ended in divorce.

Throughout both of these marriages, McGreevey ran mostly successful campaigns for office as he set his sights on the White House. He made it as far as governor of New Jersey. Also while he was getting married, divorced, fathering children, remarrying, and governing New Jersey, he spent a lot of time in bookstores and highway rest stops soliciting anonymous men for sex.

The affair that ultimately ended his political career and his second marriage was the one he had with his homeland security advisor, Golan Cipel, who had no qualifying experience for the position other than being McGreevey's lover.

Cipel is out of the picture now, and McGreevey shares a beautiful home in Plainfield, New Jersey, with his new love, Mark O'Donnell. He is also suing Dina for full custody of their daughter.

Oh yes, and he's teaching ethics at Kean University. But this isn't the end of Jimmy's story. We'll get back to him in a minute.

As I write this, my hometown's newspapers are practically oozing with the detritus of former New York governor Eliot Spitzer's political career and the utter train wreck he's created of his life as a husband and father. And for what? A twenty-two-year-old hooker from New Jersey. Not that there's anything wrong with being from New Jersey.

In the past few days we've been treated to such memorable headlines as, HO, BABY! (thank you, *New York Post*),

Pay For Luv Gov (thank you, *Daily News*), and Governors Gone Wild (nice effort, *New York Times*).

Men all over the country have been asking—desperate to know, in fact—"What in the wide world of sports can this woman do that it would cost $5,500???" and "How can I get in touch with her pimp?"

I don't think it's *what* she does that costs so much; it's *who* she does. It's about knowing that a blow job is a blow job is a blow job, but if you're paying a few thousand dollars for it, you have to convince yourself it's 275 times better than the one you got for twenty bucks behind that warehouse in the Bronx. Otherwise, you'd feel like a schmuck.

So in the space of roughly a week, a once beautiful Mrs. Spitzer aged about forty years right before our eyes (I'm sure her resplendence will return as soon as she cleans Eliot's clock in the divorce), the teenage Spitzer daughters will probably never look at men in quite the same hopeful way, a party-girl hooker will become rich and famous (for at least a few weeks), and Eliot will have to earn a living shoveling his particular brand of manure somewhere else in the world.

I wonder if he has any special talents worth $5,500 an hour?

On the bright side, the great state of New York has a brand new governor, Mr. David Paterson.

Much has been made of our new kahuna. We're constantly reminded that he's the state's first black governor and that he's the nation's first legally blind governor. And here's another "first" for the record books: He may be the first politician of any kind who, within hours of being sworn into office, told the press about all the extramarital affairs he and his wife have both already had.

Way to nip *that* sex scandal in the bud, Dave!

And—unbelievably—right on the heels of that wholesome revelation, Jim McGreevey pops his grinning face back into the news to tell the world that he and his wife had engaged in threesomes with another man, ostensibly the aide with whom McGreevey had also been having normal two-person sex, while he and Dina were still married. She, of course, denies having participated in any such adventure.

What, was McGreevey feeling left out or something? Jealous that Spitzer had a juicier sex scandal? Or that Paterson has a more progressive wife who, unlike the former Mrs. McGreevey, happily tiptoed through someone else's tulips on at least one occasion in the not-too-distant past?

Maybe we need another constitutional amendment: separation of church, state, and genitalia.

George W. Bush, who, to his credit, has never held himself up as any sort of bastion of morality, has had his fair share of unsavory sexual characters and escapades hovering in his general periphery.

There was a blogger named Jeff Gannon who, with no legitimate journalism credentials and by using a fake name, managed to get himself invited to a number of Bush's press conferences. Mr. Gannon later told the *Washington Post* about how his previous professional experience consisted mostly of pimping himself online as a gay prostitute.

Gannon had his defenders, though. Cliff Kincaid is the head of AIM (Accuracy In Media), a watchdog organization dedicated to "setting the record straight" on "botched and bungled news stories" proliferated by "the liberal news media." Of the self-outed former gay prostitute and faux reporter, Kincaid wrote, "The campaign against Gannon demonstrates the paranoid mentality and mean-spirited nature of the political left."

If it weren't for the damned liberal media, Jeff would still have a job as a fake journalist. It's terrible, I tell you. Just terrible.

In 2005, Bush nominated John Bolton as ambassador to the United Nations. This is the very same John Bolton whose first wife divorced him because he forced her to participate in group sex. She left him while he was out of town and took most of the furniture with her.

Lewis "Scooter" Libby, once George Bush's assistant and Dick Cheney's chief of staff, penned a novel in 1996 called *The Apprentice*. It was full of some of the most depraved and twisted tales in all of literature, most of them involving bestiality, incest, and pedophilia, or some combination of the three.

George's little brother, Neil, admitted in his 2003 divorce deposition that, during a business trip to Asia a few years before, he had had sex "numerous times" with a bunch of strange women. They just kept showing up in his hotel room, he said. Neil wasn't sure if the women were prostitutes, but since they never asked for money, he figured it would be okay to have sex with them anyway.

Marshall Davis Brown, the attorney representing Neil's wife, said during the deposition, "Mr. Bush, you have to admit it's a pretty remarkable thing for a man just to go to a hotel room door and open it and have a woman standing there and have sex with her."

"It was very unusual," Neil agreed.

Erudition runs in the Bush family. It runs right out the door.

The woeful tale of Republican congressman Ken Calvert of California is a classic tale of hubris and self-delusion. The man exists in a realm that exceeds his own stereotype to such a degree that it seems impossible to believe he's for real. Even more incomprehensible is that he keeps getting reelected.

Calvert was considered a champion of the Christian Coalition in those heady days in the 1990s when the term "family values" resonated throughout the nation like it meant something. Few people were more passionate in their pros- elytizing than Ken Calvert himself.

In November 1993, Calvert sat in his parked car on a Corona, California, street with a prostitute's face buried pur- posefully in his crotch.

A police officer making his late-night rounds came upon the Honorable Ken and his new little friend. The congressman pushed the hooker away, tucked his wiener back into his pants, and prepared to run. After just a few steps, he realized he would never be able to outrun the cop, not without first lopping off fifty or sixty pounds. So he stopped and decided it would be best to have a civilized conversation with the nice policeman.

For nearly a year Calvert vehemently denied all allegations that he had paid a hooker for the curbside blow job. He quieted down a bit when a local newspaper filed suit to make the police report public and won. Calvert

> "We can't forgive what occurred between the President and [Monica] Lewinsky," Calvert said, like it meant something.

explained that he had been experiencing tremendous loss and grief at the time, and the fact that he was driven into the arms (or the mouth) of another woman was mostly his ex-wife's fault. Just a few months before the incident, after fifteen years of marriage, Robin Calvert had divorced him. Furthermore, he said, he was as shocked as anyone to learn that the woman whose face was in his lap turned out to be a prostitute and a former heroin addict. Fortunately, he never got around to paying her for her services, so technically he hadn't broken any laws.

He never paid his ex-wife either. She later had to haul his considerable girth back into court for unpaid alimony and child support.

But the best of Ken Calvert came out in 1995, when his indignant voice joined all the others that were clamoring in good old-fashioned righteous Christian outrage over that other blow-job scandal that nearly put an end to Bill Clinton's presidential career in midterm. "We can't forgive what occurred between the President and [Monica] Lewinsky," Calvert said, like it meant something.

Georgia congressman Bob Barr, another God-fearing bastion of traditional family values and Biblical retribution, famously sponsored the Defense of Marriage Act in 1996, which had nothing to do with marriage and everything to do with the condemnation of homosexuality. The resolution sought to ban or severely restrict same-sex liaisons of every kind, particularly with regard to the question of gay marriage. In a fiery voice full of carefully rehearsed outrage, Barr proclaimed, "The flames of hedonism, the flames of narcissism, the flames of self-centered morality are licking at the very foundation of our society, the family unit."

Bob knew what he was talking about, too. He had been photographed licking whipped cream off the breasts of a couple of strippers at his own inaugural gala.

As for standing as a paragon of moral rectitude and an exemplar of marriage the way God intended it, he was a deadbeat dad to the children of his first two wives, and he paid for his second wife's abortion while he was carrying on an affair with another woman. The stripper-licking incident happened while he was married to his third wife.

One of Barr's hometown boys, attorney general Mike Bowers, represented Georgia in 1986 in a well-publicized case involving the state's sodomy laws.

Four years earlier, a young man named Michael Hardwick was minding his own business, in his own bedroom, having consensual sex with his own boyfriend. A police officer who had come to Hardwick's apartment to serve a warrant on a littering offense (they don't mess around in Georgia) observed Michael and his friend having "unnatural" relations. He immediately placed the men under arrest.

The Georgia law they had broken clearly stated, among other things, that it was illegal for people to engage in "any sexual act involving the sex organs of one person and the mouth or anus of another." A person convicted of this crime could be sentenced to up to twenty years in prison, where, as anyone will tell you, this sort of sexual activity hardly ever happens.

The case made it all the way to the U.S. Supreme Court, where—incredibly—the Georgia law was upheld and stayed on the books for another twelve years. It wasn't until 1998 that the Georgia Supreme Court finally overturned it.

Meanwhile, attorney general Mike Bowers had been cavorting with Anne Davis, a former *Playboy* bunny he had helped to "reform" by giving her a job as his personal secretary. Up until the moment Bowers publicly admitted to the ten-year extramarital affair with Anne in 1997, he was considered the Republican front-runner in the state's gubernatorial race. The admission effectively put an end to his career as attorney general and wannabe governor. Adultery, as it turns out, is also illegal in the great state of Georgia.

Yet another congressperson outraged by Clinton's shenanigans was Helen Chenowith of Idaho. In 1998, she called for the president's resignation in a campaign ad stating, "I believe that personal conduct and integrity do matter." A few days later, she admitted that she had been carrying on an extramarital affair for the past six years. But she still held herself a notch or two above Clinton. "I've asked for God's forgiveness," she said, "and I've received it."

Well, if it's *that* easy . . .

The Honorable Henry Hyde had his own wonderful tale of love. While he was overseeing Clinton's impeachment proceedings, Judge Hyde was having an affair with a married mother of three children. When her husband found out, he immediately filed for divorce.

For a while, it looked like the only politician never to have cheated on his wife was Democratic congressman Barney Frank of Massachusetts. But that was probably because he didn't have a wife. Frank was the only openly gay congressman at the time of the Clinton-Lewinsky scandal.

Frank was by no means the only gay person on Capitol Hill, but he was certainly one of the few prominent voices who had the courage and the dignity to stand up and say, "Yeah, I'm gay. So?"

Despite all the desperately indignant denials, the outrage, and all the carefully staged bouts of kicking and screaming, there are a great number of our fellow Americans and legislators who would probably have had much less media attention aimed their way if they had just taken their cues from Congressman Frank.

Then there's the granddaddy of them all, Newt Gingrich.

I wonder if his mother took one look at the mug on her newborn baby boy and intentionally gave him the name of a lizard. Deliberate or not, he certainly grew into his moniker.

I had the great misfortune of living in his district during my last few years in Georgia. One of the most miserable moments of my life was the night Gingrich won reelection in 1992. That election took place the year the state of Georgia had undergone some clever redistricting—or shamelessly Machiavellian maneuvering of the votership, depending on which side of the aisle you prefer.

Gingrich was by no means a newcomer during that election. We were all more than a little familiar with his vitriolic political ideologies and less than admirable personal antics.

True, I knew from the outset that the chances of his opponent winning were rather slim, but still I hoped. Newt's challenger was Ben Jones, who came to fame as an affable moonshine-drinking redneck mechanic named "Cooter" on that idiotic television show *The Dukes of Hazzard*. I clenched my teeth and tried not to throw up as I pulled the lever for Cooter. No matter what else happened, I told myself, Jones could not do nearly the amount of damage to this country as Gingrich had already wrought.

That election night, the news stations began reporting that Newt had beaten Cooter by a 60–40 margin. I remember standing by the front window of my house, looking out on the twinkling lights shining in so many other homes in Georgia's sixth congressional district. I slowly came to a rather frightening realization: I was beginning to understand what must have been going through General Sherman's head when he marched through Atlanta during the Civil War and decided to light a match. Sixty percent of my neighbors and fellow constituents had chosen a lizard to represent us. Sixty percent. I wanted to burn my own house down in protest.

"We've got to get out of here!" I wailed at my husband, who I was *certain* had voted for Newt. "I can't take this anymore!"

"In another year or two," he said in his most pleasant saner-than-thou voice. He'd been saying that since our first date. That Newt-voting bastard.

Here's what nearly turns me into a homicidal maniac every time I remember that Newt Gingrich ever represented me: It was well known for many years that Gingrich asked his first wife for a divorce as she lay in a hospital bed recovering from cancer surgery. With the ink on the divorce documents still

sticky, he married his second wife in 1981. He later divorced that one so he could marry the younger and prettier congressional aide with whom he had been having a torrid affair. And in the intervening years, Gingrich masterminded what some of us would come to think of as "The Contract on America," in which the call to bring religious values into our national politics was frighteningly like the policies of those very countries we arrogantly accuse of not "getting" democracy. And, let us not forget, it was Newt Gingrich who led the charge against the impeachment of Bill Clinton on the grounds that God doesn't approve of exposed penises in the Oval Office— or sex of any kind, for that matter—or of presidents who lie to Newt Gingrich. We should also make a small note of the comments made by one of Newt's former campaign workers, a young lady named Anne Manning, who admitted publicly that she had given Mr. Speaker a blow job or two of his own while he was still married to his first wife.[11]

Clinton's biggest problem—aside from being a lousy husband—seems to have been that he was a member of the wrong party. If not for his damned liberal agenda, he might have been great hang-out buddies with the God-fearing, stripper-licking, aide-screwing Republicans.

When you step back a bit and see the whole forest instead of focusing on the one raggedly little diseased tree everybody's talking about, it almost makes what Bill and Monica did look like a Sunday stroll in the park.

Still, they all make me want to take a scalding hot shower.

---

[11] Ewww.

After years of relative silence, Gingrich recently briefly popped back onto the national stage to make an appearance on CNN's *Larry King Live.* He was plugging his new book, *Rediscovering God in America,* and coyly suggesting that he might run for president on the Republican ticket in 2008.

Somebody fetch me my lighter.

Afterword

> Just remember,
> there's a right way and a
> wrong way to do everything,
> and the wrong way is to keep
> trying to make everybody
> else do it the right way.
>
> —"Colonel Potter" on M*A*S*H

As metaphors go, few are more beautifully succinct—or bitchy—than "Why buy the cow when you can get the milk for free?"

I find this expression particularly unsettling when it comes dripping like artificially sweetened acid from the lips of a prim woman. It always makes me want to ask her, "So, in your relationship . . . you're the cow?"

I don't know a whole lot about cows. There weren't very many of them in my old neighborhood in the Bronx, but I did grow up hearing rumors that there might be some in New Jersey, and maybe even Upstate. I was almost an adult the first time I saw a live one up close.

That cow was a lot bigger than I imagined, no prettier than I expected, and her natural fragrance was, well, not exactly elegant. Yet I found myself moved to something like pity, looking into those big, moony, not-too-bright eyes. Was it a blessing, I wondered, that she was too dumb to notice that there was a whole wide world out there that she'd never know? That her whole life was about standing there (or lying there), chewing grass and waiting to be milked? It must certainly have been a blessing to the farmer, not having to chase her or hit her over the head with a shovel before being able to collect his bucket of milk. But I'm not so sure about that cow.

What I did learn that day was that, if the farmer slacks off and neglects to milk her, she suffers for it. Milking brings her relief. And relief, in my experience, is almost always a pleasurable thing. If it's anything like driving down an interstate highway with a full bladder and seeing the sign that says NEXT REST STOP—42 MILES, then I can totally relate.

I had occasion to make my peace with that terrible old maxim at a recent family gathering, when I sat next to an Old Aunt who used to like me. She asked how things were going with "the new guy."

I smiled good-naturedly at Ella and explained that he wasn't exactly "new" anymore. First of all, we're neither one of us what you might call spring chickens. Secondly, we've been together a couple of years now, and we long ago lost our shyness about revealing all the things one tends to hide coyly at the beginning of a new relationship, like his gassiness and my predilection for enormous grandma panties.

"It's that level of comfort I love most about our relationship," I explained.

"Oh." She tried hard to look amused.

Raising a teacup to her lips, she paused momentarily and half-whispered, "Are there any plans yet?"

"Plans?" I said, looking as moony-eyed and dumb as that long-ago cow.

"Yes, plans. You can't go steady forever now, can you?"

Actually, I believe we can.

You see, I think Katharine Hepburn got it exactly right when she said that men and women should never live together; they should just visit each other every now and then. I'd probably still be married to the first guy if we had never bought that house together.

"Nope. No plans," I said, glancing toward the bar and wishing for a nice Slurpee-size cup of Tanqueray and tonic.

"Well. It must not be that serious, then." I couldn't tell whether Ella was relieved, disappointed in my lack of female cunning or moral propriety, or somehow smugly satisfied that she had been correct in her judgments of me after all.

"No," I ventured with the full knowledge that I was walking into a live minefield, "I wouldn't say it isn't serious. We're actually quite happy with the way things are. When that's no longer the case, maybe we'll try something different."

I am painfully aware that the way in which I choose to live and love tends to confuse people like Ella. In her vision of the world, a woman is born, a woman is married, and (hopefully) a woman gives birth to more women, who will then go on to perpetuate the cycle of life and continue to ensure the existence of humans on Earth from now until infinity, or until Jesus returns, whichever comes first. Men are important in Ella's Theory of the Way Things Are Supposed to Be, but only because God and Woman exist to guide them down the proper path, and because, I guess, *somebody* has to carry the luggage. I believe this is why she has been married to the same sorrowful man for nearly fifty years.

She sighed and lifted the cup to her lips again. "Well, dear, you know what they say. Why buy the cow . . ."

And there it was. She called me a cow.

That whole horridly vivid metaphor, clever as it may be, assumes that the farmer is the only one who profits from the arrangement, and that the cow is either too stupid or too complacent to see it any other way. The fact of the matter is that the farmer has to do *some* work to get the milk, not to mention provide food and shelter for her. It also completely disregards the fact that the cow actually enjoys being milked on a regular basis, especially considering the alternative, which would be to . . . what? Do it herself? Explode?

It's the partnership, not the ownership, that makes that relationship work.

Looking around this roomful of relatives, I saw quite a few women about whom all the Old Aunts had whispered at one time or another. There was one on the other side of the room, now a well-loved, wisecracking grandmother who, in her riotous adolescence, once ran away with a carnival ride operator. And over there was another, married five times, at least two of which were known to be legal. She was sitting right next to yet another who, by one of those phenomenal accidents of nature, had miraculously produced a ten-pound premature baby, just six and a half months after her fairy-tale white wedding.

I tried really hard to remember if I had ever actually met anyone with a "normal" marriage, in the way Old Aunts like Ella define "normal." In our plentiful family tree and its copious, far-reaching branches, there are wagonloads of strange fruit. Were all the women virgins when they got married? Of course not. Were all the husbands saintly? Please. Did anyone ever discover a wicked little kink in her own sexuality and follow it to its natural conclusion, secretly or otherwise? Or organize a van full of sisters to beat the living crap out of the alleged mistress of one of their husbands? Yes, yes, and yes. Was there never a creatively fabricated "where did we come from" story? There's no other way to explain how I ended up with three grandmothers. Was there love? Always.

Deep in my heart, I cheer for them all, the alleged normal ones and the happy few who refuse to be anything so ordinary. I raise my glass to the beauty, the folly, and the joyful recklessness of surrendering at long last to love, in whatever form it comes.

I turned my glance back to the woman sitting next to me. I took a deep breath, invited kindness into my heart, and said as affably as I could, "Moooove over, Aunt Ella, and let me tell you what I know about you."

Sources

ABC News

The Age (Melbourne, Australia newspaper)

AIM (Accuracy in Media)

Al-Madinah (Saudi Arabian newspaper)

AM New York (newspaper)

American Journal of Psychiatry

The Ann Arbor News (Michigan)

The Arab American (newspaper)

Asian News International

Associated Press

Atlanta Journal-Constitution

Autopsy 6: Secrets of the Dead (HBO series)

BBC News

The Birmingham Mail (England)

The Birmingham Post (England)

The Bismarck Tribune (North Dakota)

Canadian Bride magazine

CBS News

Chicago Reader

Chicago Tribune

CNN

Columbia Encyclopedia

Columbia News Service

Court TV Crime Library

Craigslist

Daily India (Madhya Pradesh newspaper)

The Daily Mail (London)

The Daily Mirror (London)
The Daily Record (Glasgow, Scotland)
The Daily Telegraph (Australian newspaper)
Denver Rocky Mountain News
The Economist
Encyclopaedia Britannica
First Coast News
Forbes Magazine
Fox News
German Press Agency
Gorkhapatra Sansthan (state-run daily newspaper of Nepal)
The Guardian (UK newspaper)
The Huffington Post
IMDB (Internet Movie Database)
The Independent (London)
The Journal News (Lower Hudson Valley, New York)
Journal of Criminal Law and Criminology
Jupiter Research
KARE-11 (NBC News affiliate, Minnesota)
Knight-Ridder Tribune
The Knot Magazine
KOB-TV News (NBC affiliate, Albuquerque, New Mexico)
The Liverpool Daily Post and Echo
The Livingston Daily (Michigan)
The Mail Today (UK newspaper)
Marketing Vox
Media Development (World Association for Christian
    Communication)
Metro News (Canada)

Metropolitan Museum of Art, New York City

The Mirror (London)

MSNBC News Services

The National Catholic Reporter

National Geographic

NBC News

Nerve magazine

New York Daily News

New York Post

New York Times

Newsweek

NPR (National Public Radio)

Orlando Sentinel

The Palm Beach Post

PBS

People magazine

The People (London)

The Pittsburg Tribune-Review (newspaper)

Reuters

Rolling Stone magazine

Salon.com

The San Francisco Chronicle

Sky News

Smithsonian Institution

The Smoking Gun

Snopes.com

Song Without Words: The Photographs and Diaries of Countess Sophia Tolstoy by Leah Bendavid-Val. National Geographic Books, 2007.

Spiegel Online International News Service

The Sun (UK)

The Sunday Independent (London)

The Sunday Mail (Glasgow, Scotland)

The Sunday Mercury (Birmingham, England)

The Sunday Mirror (London)

The Taipei Times

The Telegraph (India)

The Telegraph (UK)

Time magazine

The Tribine (Chandigahr, India)

Undying Love by Ben Harrison. St. Martin's Press, 2001.

U.S. News and World Report

USA Today

The Washington Post

Western Mail (Cardiff, England)

Women Who Love Men Who Kill by Sheila Isenberg. Simon
& Schuster, 1991.

*. . . and the roughly fourteen hundred maniacs I count among
my most cherished friends, relatives, past and present in-
laws, and all permutations thereof.*

About the Author

Cynthia Ceilán has been a professional writer, editor, and researcher since 1985. She's had short works of fiction published in *Potpourri* and *The Sun* and wrote regularly for an alternative monthly periodical called *Aquarius: A Sign of the Times* in the 1990s. She is the author of *Thinning the Herd: Tales of the Weirdly Departed*. She lives in New York City.